Praise for...

An Unguarded Moment

*"Ann Jeffries does an excellent job of weaving her characters'
stories together and keeping the reader captivated."*
—Nancy Engle, Author *Murder at Mount Joy*

*"Ann has a terrific voice for romance—it [is] light, readable
and the characters were a lot of fun."*
—Kara Cesare, the Richard Curtis Literary Agency

*"I loved the story line! A little suspenseful, which I like.
The story flowed and it felt like I was reading a movie.
I enjoyed the book."* —Gina, an avid reader

*"An engrossing and sensuous love story that immediately
grabs your attention and keeps you involved till the last page."*
—Abraham Leib, Esq.

*"My overall view is that this is a good, intelligent read! It's the
kind of story you never want to end."*
—Janice Sims, Author *This Winter Night*

*"I really admire Ann's smooth writing style and the
appealing premise of this project."*
—Mavis Allen, Associate Senior Editor, Silhouette Books

Uncommon Choices

*"Ann Jeffries has given us a great adventure and a terrific love
story together with characters who immediately come alive and
involve us in their searing passion and heartbreaking dilemmas."*
—Abe Leib, Esq.

Northern Exposures

"Ms. Jeffries never writes a slow read. Her novels are impossible to put down. I can't wait for the next installment of her Wisdom of the Ancestors Series."
—Trisha Moriarty, Author, *The Secrets She Kept*

Another Point of View

"Ann Jeffries has done it again! Once you start reading, you won't be able to put the book down!"
– J. A. Meinecke, Author of *A Woman to Reckon With*

Southern Exposures

"Loved the way [Ann Jeffries] described the activities... I felt as though I was there witnessing everything [that she was] describing. [She] immediately got my attention with the colorful... attention to details. The book is very warm. The characters have to face challenges and each does it in a different way. Loved the focus on loving family—members of the family loving each other and believing in each other." —Brenda Irons LeCesne, Esq.

"There are a lot of promising plots within the story. I thoroughly enjoyed...this [novel]. I think [Ann Jeffries'] ability [to] create emotion is a true talent. [She] did a great job creating suspense. The [characters'] stories seemed most authentic and entertaining. Language and dialogue [o]ver all... are strong areas for [Ann]."
—Karen R. Thomas, President, Creative Minds Book Group

"I always like a happy ending and being the romantic that I am the ending makes me want the continuation to be available for me to see the two characters Vivian and Benny to have the happy ending like KJ with the respective characters Chuck and Stacy."
—Sharon Jarrett-Brown, Arora Reading Group, Pittsburg, Pennsylvania.

Touch Me In The Morning

"I could not put my iPad down once I started reading. Loved the characters and story line which kept me guessing what was going to happen next."
—Pauline, an avid reader.

"Ms. Jeffries has given us a love story about two adults who, having experienced some of life's darker moments, fall deeply and passionately in love. Her characters are real life and enable the reader to eagerly ride along with them on their adventure."
—Abraham Leib, Critic.

"I loved this novel; many times finding myself lost in their lives. The author did a fantastic job with character and plot development, and an unpredictable storyline."
—Jessica Tilles, Author of *Loving Simone*

"Ann Jeffries puts so much into a book [and] pays special attention to characterization so that by the time you finish reading one of her stories you feel you know the characters. Ms. Jeffries handles the romance between Satarah and Doug with realism and with passion. You really believe they're falling in love. Satarah makes him a part of her big, loving family, a multicultural clan that will steal your heart."
—Janice Sims, best-selling author of *Thief of My Heart*

Another Family Reunion Novel
In the Wisdom of the Ancestors Series

Moments to REMEMBER

Ann Jeffries

Published and Distributed By
New View Literature
820 67th Avenue N, #7603
Myrtle Beach, South Carolina 29572
www.newviewliterature.com

Cover and Interior design: www.TWASolutions.com

ISBN: 978-0-9915003-4-5 Print
ISBN: 978-1-941603-56-7 eBook
Library of Congress Control Number: 2014909730

First printing
September 2015
Second printing December 2016
Third printing February 2017

Acknowledgements

I bow in humble gratitude to:

The Creator

The Ancestors

Jessica Tilles, Editor

Abe Leib, Esq., for many things great and small

The Carolina Forest Writers' Group

My family, friends, and fans

The journey continues and the struggle for

literary perfection shall never end.

I remain faithfully yours,

Ann Jeffries

Other Titles

In the Family Reunion—Wisdom of the Ancestors Series

Southern Exposures

Another Point of View

Northern Exposures

Uncommon Choices

An Unguarded Moment

Touch Me In The Morning

Like the sands through the hour glass

So are the days of our lives

And for that live moment we thrive

Awakenings, as we make the dead come alive

Rise and walk...come into the light

– Socrates

Prologue

THE SAND WAS HOT, EVEN IN the shadow of Ship Rock Mountain, a tubular edifice that spiraled upward into the blazing blue sky. No wind, no rain cooled the air and the heat burned all vegetation since time immortal. Yet, the voices danced on air as if in some native ballet partnered with the waves of heat on the vast horizon. The tongue and tone of the voices were foreign, not of this world. Strangely, the air carried stillness, a pause that obeyed the sounds.

Far in the distance, a bright light shone like a flash that grew in hue and brilliancy like a trapped aurora borealis. As it came closer to the mountain, it grew in intensity and beauty. Moving without disturbing the air or touching the hot ground, shortly the light was all-encompassing, blocking the sun and devouring the heat in its changing, calming turquoise glow. Pure light cooled, and comfort began to take on a shape. Out of the light, a woman stood, her face beautiful, her long, thick, black hair like hot, wet asphalt blowing in some surreal wind, her arms extended, beckoning as if to embrace. She had eyes the color of a doe's pelt and a smile so engaging it was purely memorizing.

The voice was a siren's song on the gentle turquoise air, warm and enchanting.

"It is time, my love. Look to your own heart. Feel it beat for another. Gather close those who have strayed. All will return to you and another will come. Farewell, my love, for I will come to you no more."

Jake Hawkins' eyes opened and his arms reached out to the dream that vanished. He uttered one word with an agonizingly sweet pain. "Skai."

Chapter One

JAKE HAWKINS SAT NUDE ON THE side of his leather-covered sleigh bed, his elbows on his knees, and palms of his hands slowly rubbing his face. It was 4:20 A.M. on the day of his daughter's, JaiHonnah's, wedding. A dream—so real that perspiration still beaded his powerful frame—awakened him.

He was not a fanciful man, not one to believe overmuch in dreams, mystical aberrations or a hereafter. With no promise of tomorrow, he believed he had to do his living while he was alive. So, he lived well, enjoying the fruits of his labor. At fifty years of age, there wasn't much he hadn't done several times over, of which not all of those things made him proud. Nevertheless, he didn't wake up each day with regrets. He had the wealth and resources to do nearly anything and everything he wanted. He built an empire from near nothing. He came from strong, unadulterated slave stock. His father, Hudson, was a tall, husky man, black as tar and strong as steel. He was descended from escaped slaves who lived in the Louisiana bayou, undetected for generations.

Stolen from their homeland of Barbados, his mother's ancestors were forced to work in fish canaries for generations. His mother, Joule, was fifteen when a hurricane blew through Louisiana and destroyed much of its commerce. Joule's mother died during the storm and a poisonous snake killed her father. Destitute, confused, and injured, Joule stumbled into the bayou where a clan of former slaves, including Hudson Hawkins, found her.

Though slavery had ended more than one hundred years earlier, vestiges of the Old South kept the wages low for people of color. Joule found a different life in the wilds of the swamplands, married Hudson, a man who spoke in a thick Cajun dialect, and bore him two children: Jake and Mavis.

As civilization edged closer into the bayou, Joule insisted her children attend school. Little did she know that was the beginning of the end for the family of four. Inoculated against childhood diseases before they could attend the one-room Parish school closest to them, Jake was fourteen and Mavis only eleven when their parents died of a disease that didn't affect the inoculated children. Jake and Mavis were taken from their clan and forced into an orphanage. When Mavis complained to Jake about physical and sexual abuse by a male attendant, Jake caught the man alone, unaware, and beat him to within an inch of his life. He didn't much care whether the man lived or died from the beating. Jake took Mavis and escaped that same dark night through the bayou. Not wanting to endanger others in their community, they accepted provisions and struck out going westward.

With a ninth-grade education, the clothes on their backs, and knowledge of the bayou, Jake Hawkins and his sister eluded the Parish Sheriff and hit the road on foot, headed for California. On their way, hitchhiking when they could, walking when they couldn't, they hitched a ride with Ezra Neal, a twenty-four-year-old man, in his battered, old extended-cab pickup truck. Ezra was heading for the Texas oil fields to work his trade as a well digger. Hearing their story, Ezra took Jake and Mavis along on his journey, shared his meager funds, and bought them food and clothing. They often had to sleep in the truck and wash up at a truck stop in the morning.

Jake, big and strong for his age, learned to work the oil fields and Ezra put Mavis in school, claiming she was his niece. When Mavis was older, she got babysitting jobs in the community of oil workers. Jake, Mavis, and Ezra lived simply by pooling their savings.

At seventeen years old, an oilrig accident in Galveston put Jake in the hospital where he met Skai Littlefeather, a twenty-one-year-old Navajo nurse. Six months later, Jake and Skai were married in a traditional Native American ceremony on the Navajo Reservation in Ship Rock, New Mexico. When they returned to Galveston after their marriage, the oil company paid the out-of-court accident claim. Jake had more money than he had ever dreamed of, but the oil company's insurance carriers' questions about Jake's background and age caused Ezra, Jake, Skai, and Mavis to take the money and leave Galveston before a full-blown investigation could begin.

A week later, after stopping on the road for a meal, the foursome were leaving San Antonio heading north and west toward Skai's family's home in Ship Rock when Jake spotted a dilapidated government FOR SALE sign advertising an old plantation. Jake detoured, taking a dilapidated, long road, driving Ezra's old battered truck over broken concrete with weeds sprouting in the cracks and crevices for more than seventy miles. They passed deserted homes that weren't much more than huts, old houses where people lived eking out an existence with chickens or hogs and vegetable patches, and trailer homes in communities with dirt roads and no names. There was no water or sewer system. Wells, rain barrels, and septic systems served the area. Propane gas was used for cooking and windmills provided electricity. The land was sparsely populated with people originally from Mexico, Native Americans, and others who were similarly down-on-their-luck. Though the land was dirt cheap, it was too desolate and too far from San Antonio to interest developers.

When they reached their destination, what Jake saw at the center of the dispiriting scenery, was a three-story ramshackle antebellum mansion with decaying outbuildings that at some point in the distant past must have been a thriving plantation with hundreds of workers and thousands of acres surrounding it. When he stepped down from the old truck that had brought him from his Louisiana bayou, he knew he was home. Jake bought the land with the money from his accident settlement and began to build his empire.

Jake stood up and walked out of his huge bedroom suite into his private, glass-enclosed solarium. The light in the eastern sky was dim in graduating shades of gray. Yet he could see the acres of dewy, green grass surrounding his home; hear the wranglers beginning to move his herds of cattle from one pasture to graze in another. The whinnies and neighing came from his thoroughbreds and wild horses quaking, trembling waiting for his foremen to begin mating the animals to further improve the bloodlines. Further away, workers would be testing the water in his hydroponics farms or harvesting the fruits and vegetables for markets both near and far and some of the produce would be consumed at his daughter's wedding. Fresh flowers would be cut and used as table arrangements in the ballroom. In the town he built, Hawkinstown, families would be readying their children for the Saturday school at the fully-equipped library he also built. He heard the sound of one of his planes from BlackHawk Air bringing in the mail, magazines, newspapers, and supplies for his general stores. Later, other planes would bring in guests for his daughter's wedding.

Jake, out of sensitivity for his houseguests' sensibilities, dressed in a robe and short drawstring pants, freshened up and walked half the length of his eighteen-thousand-square-foot house with six-thousand-square-feet on the main level alone to the kitchen. When he entered, he found Ezra Neal kissing his mother-in-law, Kiavi Littlefeather, against the refrigerator. He cleared his throat loudly before moving toward the coffee urn.

"Boy, ain't chew learnt to leave a man in peace when he's sparkin' a woman?" Ezra asked, exasperated.

"You've been trying to hug up on that ol' woman for years. If you ain't lit her fire by now, no amount of sparking is gonna get you some love," Jake said, lazily, his Texas accent apparent.

"Look to your own heart, Jake Hawkins," Kiavi Littlefeather said, unashamed, something unfathomable in the depth of her obsidian eyes.

Look to your own heart. Jake remembered the words from his dream and stared at Kiavi, Skai's mother. Looking at her was like looking at an older version of his deceased wife. Both women were small in stature, but strong in will. Though Kiavi's hair was still mostly black, it was streaked liberally with gray. Had Skai lived, she would have been fifty-five years old. Though Kiavi had to be into her late sixties or early seventies, her smooth, unwrinkled face could have been mistaken for a woman half that age. Jake saw many similarities to Kiavi in his daughter's beautiful face. JaiHonnah's beauty won her first runner up in the Ms. America

Pageant. What he contributed to his daughter's appearance was her height and a little cocoa to her café-au lait complexion. The high cheekbones, whiskey colored eyes, and long, black silky hair came from his wife's Navajo, Apache, and Spanish ancestries.

Kiavi's hands on Jake's arms brought him back from his musings. She looked up into his eyes, searching for what he did not know, but she found whatever it was, smiled gently, and then walked away to continue her task. It took a moment more of remembrances for Jake to pour coffee into the cup and then sit at the long, trestle, kitchen table.

Ezra sat across from him with his hands wrapped around his own cup. "What you studdin', boy?" Ezra asked.

Jake shook his head, distancing himself from his thoughts and then asked, "Why are you up so early? It's barely five o'clock."

"Stubborn woman wanted to make her own breakfast before the caterers got here to start the family's breakfast and prepare for JaiHawk's weddin'. Couldn't convince her to come back to bed," he groused. He finished his coffee and rose from the table. He was still a strong, sturdy, man with a scruffy beard. His eyes, for a man his age, were sharp and assessing. "Might as well get to doin' since I'm up." With one last hopeful look in Kiavi's direction,

Ezra left the kitchen for his bedroom suite on the northern front of the mansion.

Ezra managed the house and the ranch and worked every day from can't see in the morning to can't see at night. For a man sixty plus years old, he showed no signs of slowing down. He was respected by the two hundred or more ranch hands and was shown deference by those he did business with to buy and sell livestock and crops. Though his wealth was considerable after working with Jake for many years, his only possession was a small house he built in the mountains near a lake with good fishing and quiet surroundings.

Though Ezra loved Jake's children as if they were his own grandchildren, once he met Kiavi, he never married or had children of his own. Still, he was a complete and fulfilled man.

Kiavi put a freshly baked loaf of fry bread on the table and sat down in the seat Ezra vacated with her cup of tea and fresh fruit. She cut the fruit and began to eat. "You had a vision," she said simply.

Jake plucked a cigarillo from his breast pocket, struck a wind match with his thumbnail and lit it while eying Kiavi. "I had a dream."

"You had a vision; a visitation."

"Whatever," Jake said, dismissively.

"My child has been with the ancestors for twenty summers. Your second child has been missing for longer. Jacob Junior is thirty-four. LaiLoni Skai is thirty-three, Adam thirty-two and JaiHonnah is thirty-one. She would not have wanted you to grieve her loss this many summers. You were not built to live alone."

Lately he had to admit, at least to himself, he had another woman on his mind.

He first met Kelley Baylor at the offices of Baylor Construction. He went there to size up one of her brothers, J. Roderick Baylor, the former basketball icon JRock cum businessman. What he found when he entered the business office was far more than he had bargained for.

The brown-eyed beauty, looking like a full-bodied Dorothy Dandridge, with a full head of real hair, who sat on the edge of a desk swinging one perfectly-shaped leg, made Jake's mouth water. He took advantage of his dark sunglasses to cover her entire torso with one, long searing gaze. Smooth cinnamon-brown skin, full dark hair, and the eyes of an angel or a devil. He settled his gaze on her full, luscious mouth that parted just slightly. His eyes moved down to her full bosom and narrowing waist. It was the lazy sway of her hips as she approached that caused him to chew hard on his cigar. *This was a woman!* he thought at the time. No silly little bright-eyed youngster who didn't know diddly-squat about a man. This one had seasoning, style, and most of all class. He checked quickly for a wedding band.

"I'm Kelley Baylor. May I be of assistance?"

"You already have, little lady," Jake had grinned, *"but I'll get to that later. Now, where's the boy?"*

"Well, if you're into that kind of trade; young male prostitutes hang out around DuPont Circle in Northwest. You'd probably find better around San Francisco. That's a ways west of here," she quipped. *"Thataway."* She motioned with her thumb over her right shoulder toward the west.

A thumb and forefinger kicked up Jake's Stetson. He leaned in close to her, stuck a cheroot between his pearl-white teeth, and popped a wind match with his thumbnail, eyeing her closely as it lit. *"Concerned about my sexual proclivities, are you, dahlin?"*

Kelley puckered her kissable, red lips and sensuously blew out the match. *"You want to light up something, cowboy, take it outside."*

"I aim to do just that, dahlin, soon as I straighten out a little business. You be here when I get back. Tell the boy I'm here," he said ascending the wide, center staircase with his eyes still on her.

Kelley's eyes followed his departure up the staircase. *"Oh, I think you'll find him soon enough on your own. Where should I send your remains?"*

Jake grinned and continued up the steps behind his two men.

When he descended the steps a while later, he met Kelley's smug, sexy grin and sassy stance, with her arms akimbo.

"Find what you were looking for, cowboy?"

"I see you're still waiting for me."

"I was waiting for the undertaker so he could haul your carcass outta here after JRock got finished ballin' on that Stetson."

"Don't nobody touch my Stetson, little lady. I do everything in this hat."

"Must be a tight squeeze with you and your ego under that hat band."

"You'll find out just how tight at dinner tonight."

"Really? When?"

"Six o'clock. Where?"

"The Omni at eight."

"Atlanta?"

"You've heard of it, I see."

"You'll see a lot more by ten o'clock."

"Bring your spurs, cowboy. It's gonna be a rough ride."

Jake grinned. Yep, he was beginning to like these Baylors—a lot.

Since that first meeting, Kelley Baylor led him on a merry chase, but he was letting her have her head while he continued to reel her in inch by inch. Soon she would run out of real estate and he'd have her right where he wanted her.

Chapter Two

IT DIDN'T MATTER THAT THE SUN was not shinning or that the rain was pouring in buckets. The thunder roared and the lightening flashed. The gray-to-black clouds hung low in the Texas sky just above a distant ridge. The raindrops beat against the windows, obscuring the view of the south lawn as the wind picked up in gusts. The gurgling water draining from the roof into the rain barrels played along with Mother Nature's tunes.

The candles flickered slightly and the light created a warm glow to the expansive solarium. The potted plants, strategically placed throughout the ballroom, spread sweet fragrances in the ceiling-fan-driven air. The round tables covered in crisp, white, damask tablecloths with canary-yellow skirts scalloped and ruffled at the edges and overlaid with the finest, handmade, white, eyelet lace billowing onto the highly shined, blond, hardwood floor were a study in loveliness. Scented candle centerpieces in varying heights on pewter holders laced with green ivy, baby's breath, and a perfusion of yellow roses were surrounded by hand-hammered, pure silver plates topped with fine bone china. The silver edges of the plates rimmed the ornate "H" intertwined with an image of a fearsome, but regal hawk, as it lifted with wings unfurled. A trio of Waterford crystal goblets, with a matching hand-honed etched design, sat above the plates and caught the glow of the candles. The silverware, too, had the Hawkins' crest embedded in the handle. Bright, yellow, linen napkins stood crisp and looked as if they, like the hawk, might take flight at any moment.

A baby whined in the background and someone coughed. They, along with over two hundred others, were there to witness the event, but it did not matter. The centerpiece of everyone's rapt attention could have been completely alone with her man and she wouldn't have been happier.

He took her hand in his and she looked up into his earth-shattering smile. His dark eyes shining and causing a rush of electric energy to flow through her. It was like the first time they met more than a year ago. His brawn and virility captured her. His kisses and caresses seduced her. His arms held her in sweet ecstasy. His words and deeds captivated her. Now their words sealed their bond.

"By the power vested in me by the State of Texas, I pronounce you, John Roderick Baylor, and you, JaiHonnah Reise Hawkins, to be husband and wife. What The Creator has joined together let no man put asunder. You may kiss your bride," the Justice of the Peace said, smiling.

Roderick looked into JaiHonnah's smiling eyes and knew a new life was beginning for him. He kissed the palms of her hands, the wedding band on the third finger of her left hand, and then took her into his arms.

"I love you, Jai," he whispered, as he planted a mesmerizing kiss on her lips. "I'm in love for the last time in my life."

"And I'm in love for the first time in my life," she said and smiled sincerely.

They kissed again tenderly, longingly, and deeply amid loud cheers and applause. JaiHonnah's words caused an explosion of heat in Roderick's groin. He was so deeply in love he was oblivious to the commotion surrounding them. Looking into his bride's beautiful face made his temperature rise and his desire for her showed fiercely. It seemed everything, but the sparkle in her topaz eyes, ceased to exist.

"Well, boy, welcome to my family." Jake Hawkins grinned, slapping Roderick on the back.

Roderick didn't turn his face away from his new bride. "Welcome to *my* family, old man," he said, grinning. "If you behave yourself, we won't put you up for adoption."

"Then you can just unhand my daughter and we can get this marriage annulled fast as a prairie dog's tail can flick," he said, grinning back, possessively slipping his arms around his daughter's narrow waist.

"Oh, no, Daddy, there will be no annulment of this marriage." JaiHonnah smiled into Roderick's eyes. "I've got the only love and life I want, but you'll always be my daddy." She smiled up at her father.

Jake embraced his daughter in a tight hug. "You'll always be my JaiHawk." He kissed both of her cheeks. "Remember that. You can always come home."

"Not this time, Daddy," JaiHonnah whispered for her father's ear only. "Roderick loves me for me, not because I'm your daughter and not for any financial or political gain he thinks he will receive."

"He's a dead man walking, if he hurts you," Jake whispered back.

JaiHonnah froze at the chill in her father's voice. Jake Hawkins never made idle threats. He would, could, and had destroyed business empires with far less provocation than someone thinking of hurting her. Her former husband and father-in-law could bear witness to Jake's vehemence and rued the day they had ever laid eyes on her.

"Save some of that for me and the rest of the Baylors," Kelley Baylor beamed, as she reached for her new sister-in-law and tightly hugged her. "You look radiant, Jai, and so do you, JRock." She kissed her brother and held him tightly. "You two will be very happy together."

"Thanks, Kelley," JaiHonnah said, smiling. "I've never been so happy." She laid her head back against her husband's wide, firm chest and he engulfed her in a warm embrace.

Roderick bent and kissed JaiHonnah's ear. "Neither have I," he whispered.

JaiHonnah angled her neck to look up at him over her shoulder. His mouth reached hers eagerly and gently.

"You two have a lifetime for that." Walter Baylor, Roderick and Kelley's oldest brother, laughed, hugging his wife, Marie, at her waist. "That kind of action led Marie and me to have seven kids."

"You bragging or complaining?" Roderick laughed good-heartedly at his brother. He temporarily released his hold on JaiHonnah to embrace his sister-in-law.

"No brag, just facts." Marie smiled in Roderick's embrace. "You two be happy, you hear me?"

"They couldn't miss," a voice came, widening the circle around Roderick and JaiHonnah.

"Hi, Sis, I'm glad you could make it." Roderick smiled, as he kissed another of his sisters, Karen Baylor Knight. "Did you bring Harold and the children with you?"

"You didn't give me much time, little brother." Karen smiled, though he towered over her at six-foot-seven, by at least a foot. "Yes we're all here. We didn't have much choice either, now did we?" she teased.

"Sorry, Karen, but it's not often you get to witness a miracle." Roderick eased his arm around JaiHonnah's waist again. "When this beautiful lady said she would marry me, I wasn't about to give her time to change her mind."

"Maybe she should have thought about it again before she made another mistake! How much is this one going to cost the family, Jai?"

The air of joy stilled and all heads turned toward the sharp reproach.

"Jacob!" JaiHonnah flashed. "You are my brother and I love you, but I resent your speaking to or about Roderick that way. He is my husband now, the man I love, and a member of our family. You will respect him."

Jacob's strong jaw muscle flexed and his stunningly handsome, golden-brown face darkened. His thick, curly, black hair fell just below his shoulders and tied with a thin rawhide, twined at the nape of his neck. Magnificent physique, high cheekbones, and raven-black eyebrows evidenced his combined African American-Spanish-Navajo-Apache ancestry and afforded him a powerful masculine presence.

"The way he respected you!" he shot back sharply. "Last Christmas you came home in tears, pregnant with this bastard's seed in your body! He wanted nothing to do with you then, but now, suddenly, he asks you to marry him! Why do you think that is, Jai? It's not the scent of a woman that brought him here, little sister. He smells the money—"

"Jacob, I won't tolerate this from you or anyone else! What happened between me and Roderick—"

"You don't have to explain anything to him, baby!" Roderick interjected, glaring at Jacob. He stepped forward to speak directly to his new brother-in-law. "If you have something to say to me, Hawkins, we can take this to another room, but you will *not* embarrass JaiHonnah on our wedding day or speak to my wife in that tone ever again!" Roderick hissed menacingly.

"*Your wife!*" Jacob ridiculed with disdain. "You forget who she is and where you are, Baylor! She is a Hawkins! This is my house, my town, and my rules!"

"No, *you* remember who she is! She is JaiHonnah Reise *Baylor* now and I don't give a damn about your property or your rules! The sooner my wife and I are out of this house the better!"

Jacob lowered his voice and angled closer to Roderick, whose stance stiffened to meet the challenge.

"Keep it that way! She had better not shed one tear or I'll—"

"Silence!" a stern voice parted the tense crowd.

Kiavi Littlefeather's slight frame stood regally in her traditional Navajo ceremonial attire. Her black eyes flashed over Jacob Junior and Roderick.

"*Shimá sâni—*" Jacob started, modulating his tone, instantly backing down from his stance, but not looking at her.

Kiavi did not speak immediately, but her black, piercing eyes chilled Jacob Junior. "No son of Skai, grandson of Keanu, great grandson of Ra and great, great grandson of Matese, the Spaniard, will insult another man's woman." Her voice was low, but filled with strength. "We will speak of this no more!"

As if the Eleventh Commandment were spoken, the tension instantly quelled.

Jacob Junior's head bowed slightly. He glared at Roderick and took a surreptitious glance at his grandmother's proud and impervious face. "Yes, *Shimá sâni,*" he said slightly above a whisper.

JaiHonnah gripped Roderick's arms and looked up into his staunch stare at Jacob. "Honey, please." Her eyes pleaded, as she slid her hands down his arms and laced her fingers in his.

The crowd dissipated and Roderick relaxed his stiff stance. He looked down into his wife's watery eyes. His ire melted away. "You will never regret this day, JaiHonnah. No more pain," he promised, caressing her face.

"What the *hell* was that all about?" asked Francis Baylor, Roderick's other brother. "Brotherman on the war path has a real attitude problem. Looked like he was ready to take your scalp, JRock."

"Let's just drop it, okay?" Roderick flashed.

Francis put up both hands in a show of surrender and backed away. "Okay, okay. It's your nut to crack, little brother." The term, *little brother* was a misnomer. Francis was the third child of John and Sarah Baylor, but JRock, the youngest child of the five, stood heads above all of his other siblings.

Roderick was angry, more with himself than with the accusation and threat from JaiHonnah's brother. Nevertheless, her brother spoke the truth. He recalled how just last year, a week before Christmas, he hurled accusations at her and the feeling of betrayal that gripped him. He thought he saw shades of his first wife's, Monique's, traitorous behavior in JaiHonnah and verbally lashed out at her. His villainous behavior sent JaiHonnah running in tears from his office. Running from him and his life. Now he winced at the thought of it all. He loved JaiHonnah even then, but his blind fury would not let him see JaiHonnah was nothing like Monique. His fury kept them apart for nine months before he realized JaiHonnah would not and could not hurt him in the same way Monique had done. That JaiHonnah loved him deeply and he loved her. That JaiHonnah had carried his seed in her womb when she left. His twin sons were four months old before he ever knew they existed. Replaying that scene every day enraged him for his own stupidity, but, for now, he refused to think past the moment. The miserable time away from JaiHonnah was behind them and he would never let anything or anyone come between them again.

Adam Hawkins, a younger and more handsome version of Jacob, Junior, approached.

"Jai," he said, gently touching his younger sister's shoulder.

JaiHonnah turned out of Roderick's embrace and smiled up at her brother. "Adam," she said, as she warmly hugged and kissed him on the cheek. "I'm glad you came. Daddy said that you were in Africa and probably couldn't make it home in time for the wedding."

"I just got here. Business or wild horses couldn't have kept me away, but I've already heard from Aunt Mavis that Jacob has—"

"Let's not dwell on it now. I want you to meet my husband, J. Roderick Baylor." She smiled. "Roderick, this is my other brother, Adam Clayton Hawkins."

Roderick extended his hand and Adam shook it firmly. "I remember you," Adam said, without a smile. "I followed your basketball career when you were in college, the NBA, and since then. You're quite an astute businessman, Baylor. People call you the Bill Gates of the construction industry. I understand you've bought enough shares of BlackHawk International to seat yourself on our board of directors."

"My decision to buy into BlackHawk was a tactical business move that had nothing to do with JaiHonnah," Roderick said defensively. "I don't intend to exploit my relationship with the conglomerate or your family because I'm married to the boss' daughter. She's no bargaining chip. My business and my personal life are separate entities and will not be mixed."

"I'll take it as your oath, Baylor, and give you fair warning," stated Adam. "You and my father are a lot alike. You both came from nothing and built empires. Don't make the same mistake JaiHonnah's ex-husband, Calvin Chapman, made. The Hawkins don't suffer fools lightly or benevolently."

"Neither do I, Adam," Roderick said coldly. "Neither do I."

"Can't we put business aside just for today, Adam?" JaiHonnah pleaded. "Please, honey?" She looked up into Roderick's eyes.

Roderick's granite-like expression softened, as he smiled at his wife. "Yes, this is neither the time nor the place." He nodded at Adam.

Adam returned the gesture and walked away.

"Daddy! Daddy!" Shelley and Shelby Baylor squealed joyfully.

Roderick's face brightened, as his twin, six-year-old daughters approached at the speed of light. He stooped to receive them, opening his arms. The girls raced to him, kissing his face and hugging his neck.

"Did we do it right, JaiHonnah?" Shelby asked, her innocent face full of apprehension.

JaiHonnah smiled broadly and lowered to their level. Caressing each face, she said, "Perfect. You two were beautiful little bridesmaids."

"Indian princesses, Jai," Shelley corrected affirmatively.

"Oh, yes, Indian princesses." JaiHonnah smiled and winked.

"Great Grandmother Kiavi said we have the wisdom of the ancestors in us. What does that mean, Daddy?"

Roderick was pleased with his daughters' eager acceptance of JaiHonnah's grandmother as their own, but that is how it was from the beginning. The twins accepted JaiHonnah lovingly from the first moment they met her and she returned their love in full measure.

"I'm not sure, sweetheart. Perhaps you'll have a chance to ask her while you're visiting with her on the Navajo Reservation."

"I can't wait," Shelley squealed. "Can we stay for a long, long time, Daddy?"

A smile grew around Roderick's lips. "Only a week, sweetheart. You and your sister have to get back to school, remember?"

"Aw, Daddy," Shelley whined. "Reise and Rodney don't have to get back to go to school."

"Your brothers are only five months old, Shelley. They don't go to school yet," he reasoned. "So until the boys are old enough, you and your sister will have to teach them. The more you learn the more you can teach and you learn something new every day."

"What are you and JaiHonnah going to learn on your honeymoon?" Shelby asked innocently, her expression quizzical.

Roderick covered his face, briefly stifling his urge to laugh. "Uh, we're going to learn how to answer questions like that. It's going to be a very interesting learning experience."

"You're going to tell us all about it when you get back, aren't you, Jai?" Shelley asked.

"We'll bring souvenirs back for all of you," Jai said, blushing.

"Okay, we understand." Shelby sighed. "You're going to kiss a lot and be all mushy."

"At least." Roderick grinned devilishly at JaiHonnah.

The band began to play. Roderick and JaiHonnah kissed the girls before they scampered away. Standing Roderick helped JaiHonnah to her feet. His dark eyes glowed. "May I have this dance, Mrs. Baylor?"

JaiHonnah's expression softened into a brilliant smile. "This and every dance, Mr. Baylor," she cooed. "For the rest of our lives."

Roderick took her into his arms and they swayed to the music, staring into each other's eyes and thoughts. JaiHonnah slipped her hands around Roderick's neck and felt the intensity of the heat emanating from him. His engorged phallus boldly pressed against her, making a promise of the ecstasy to come. His blatant masculinity excited her beyond belief. She felt the pangs of her need for him rising quickly, as he held her. When his mouth captured hers, she opened to his probing tongue, and together their tongues danced erotically.

Roderick groaned his need for her, as they kissed more deeply. Every fiber of his being came alive. His heart thundered in his chest, as he pulled her deeper into his embrace. He would take her right then and there if he could. Wave after wave of pleasure washed over him, building his desires. Her full breasts heaved seductively against his chest, with taut nipples protruding through the fabric of her wedding gown. Her soft, exotic scent mesmerized him, teasing his senses.

"How long do we have to stay?" he breathed heavily against her lips.

JaiHonnah inhaled her husband's enticing scent. "We have to cut the cake, sip champagne, and toss the bouquet. Of course, Daddy has laid a feast out. We'll be eating for hours."

"I don't want cake or champagne or food. I want to taste only you, Mrs. Baylor, so if you don't mind breaking with tradition, could we get the hell out of here? I've got to get you out of that dress before I go crazy."

JaiHonnah smiled devilishly. "Where do you want to take me?"

"To bed for a year or two," Roderick answered quickly.

"Then the honeymoon is over?" she asked impishly.

"That's when it begins, Mrs. Baylor, now toss those damn flowers. I've got to have you."

JaiHonnah grinned and, without looking, tossed the flowers over her head. The bouquet sailed through the air like a heat-seeking missile on a mission. Suddenly, Kelley Baylor found the bouquet hurling through the air at her and landing in her hands. The surprise showed on her face, as she watched her brother and JaiHonnah dash out of the ballroom. Her face flushed with embarrassment while the guests laughed and clapped.

Jake Hawkins stood in a practiced pose, eyeing the ballroom filled to overflowing with guests. He remained in silhouette, watching the events of the day unfolding and orchestrating most of what occurred. He liked what he saw and that knowledge brought a smile to his lips.

Recalling the time he'd spent researching J. Roderick Baylor, monitoring the growth of his businesses, and the manner in which he operated, gave him reason to be satisfied. A lesser man would have buckled under the pressure he brought to bear.

Dare he think the unthinkable? His long-held dream was beginning to take shape. He pivoted and walked to a secluded area of a salon adjoining the ballroom. Pulling a Havana Cigar from his vest pocket, he ran it under his nose, savoring the scent. He clipped the end, scratched the business end of a wind match with his thumbnail, and watched it light.

Surveying the land he held dear, he grinned while lighting the cigar. A deep, almost sinister laugh curled out with the smoke. *Men and strategy*, he thought deeply. Five years of watching the young lions honing their craft.

Vivian Jackson Montgomery, Roderick's friend and lawyer, overplayed her hand this time, he thought as he flicked away ashes from his cigar and placed it back between his teeth. Now that she was out of the way, he'd see what this J. Roderick Baylor was made of. His grin broadened. He was biding his time. He would still put pepper in the pot and let it simmer and stew. He drew the cigar from his clenched teeth again and looked at it thoughtfully.

He did not intend for his beautiful daughter to be a weapon. Her marriage to Baylor couldn't be halted without drawing too much suspicion though. His eyes were still on the prize. A clear path lay ahead. Who would ascend to the throne? Hawkins or Baylor? Who would be king of the hill? A confident smile regained prominence of his face.

"Father?" Adam interrupted, standing beside him.

"Yes, son," Jake said, still surveying a mere fraction of the landscape he had amassed in his lifetime.

"I've completed negotiations in South Africa. BlackHawk-Africa will begin its operation within the next thirty to sixty days."

"You've done well, Adam. I'm very pleased. You accomplished our goals despite your being distracted by romantic notions."

"'Notions?'" Adam snorted. "Try feelings on for size. Love even."

"All in due time, son. All in due time," Jake said thoughtfully.

"Jake, I'm thirty-two years old. I want to find someone to come home to at night. It's all well and good for you and Jacob to burn your candles at both ends, but I want more for me than that." He looked away from his father and softened his tone. "Frankly, I'm thinking about leaving BlackHawk International. Maybe starting something of my own."

"She's married, Adam. Vivian Alexander remarried a while ago."

"I know. I also know that was why you've kept me out of the country for so long, running our foreign companies and investments. You knew I was interested in her."

"It was for your own good, son."

"Father, I love you, but you manipulate us—all of us—like puppets. We all dance to your music. I'm glad to see, at least, Jai broke free."

Adam turned and started to walk away. Jake caught his arm.

"I love you too, son," he said, looking into Adam's eyes.

Adam heard the sincerity in his father's voice. He exhaled and nodded his head in acknowledgment. "I know you do, Dad. You've done your best by all of us. It still doesn't always make what you do to us right."

Jake felt the truth of his son's statement. Since someone kidnapped his daughter, LaiLoni Skai, as a newborn, he held onto his remaining three children tightly.

He refused to have regrets for his actions. He loved and protected his children fiercely. As long as there was breath in his body and a dime in his pocket, he would never change.

Later, Jake approached Kelley, and said, "Having a nice time, Ms. Baylor?" He grinned, eying the provocative décolletage of Kelley Baylor's form-fitting dress.

"Is that question directed at me or my tits, Mr. Hawkins?"

"You do say what you mean, Ms. Baylor." He grinned. "I like that kind of directness in a woman." His not-too-subtle eyes wandered over her above the rim of his glass of straight bourbon.

"With you, Mr. Hawkins, I find I'd better mean what I say."

"Uh-huh, then you've given my proposition some thought?"

"It's intriguing," she said, dispassionately looking away. "It's not every woman who is offered a million dollars to sleep with a man," she leaned in close to his ear, "but then I'm not every woman," she cooed, turning on her heels and walking away.

She glanced over her shoulder at him, gave him a Mona Lisa smile, and a full view of her lazily swaying hips, as she sashayed away.

Beads of perspiration dotted Jake's brow. He'd be damned if that female weren't the devil. She vexed him sorely. The sight of her rounded hips hardened his groin. He'd be spending more time in Atlanta. He was going to have Ms. Kelley Baylor or the moon would never shine again at night.

"You're beautiful." Roderick sighed, holding JaiHonnah in his arms, as they reclined in her bedroom suite, their thunderous union as husband and wife subsiding slightly.

"You make me feel beautiful." She sighed, kissing his bare chest and biting at his raisin-like nipples.

Roderick's body tightened from the sensation of her mouth on him. Her fingers leisurely glided over his pronounced six-pack and down his bare thigh. He sucked in his breath through gritted teeth, as her hand wandered further down between his thighs and cupped him.

"You want me to turn my head and cough, honey?" he teased.

JaiHonnah laughed. "I love to touch your body. I love the way you feel and how you taste. I enjoy making love with you."

"I'm going to make a steady diet out of you, too, Mrs. Baylor. Morning, noon and night." He smiled, positioning her nearly nude body on top of him.

JaiHonnah laid her head beside his cheek and burrowed into his embrace. She shuddered involuntarily and Roderick noticed.

"Are you cold?" He reached for the billion-count comforter, pulling it over both of them.

"We're going to be happy, aren't we, Roderick?"

There was a note of apprehension in her voice.

Roderick noticed. He angled his head so that he could look into her eyes. "What is it, Jai? What's bothering you?"

JaiHonnah leaned up and gently kissed his mouth. "It's not important."

"It is, yes. If you ask me a question like that, it's very important. I'm in love with you, Jai. I don't just hope or think we're going to be happy. I know it. We won't let it be any other way. Now, tell me, what's bothering you?"

JaiHonnah again laid her head against his cheek and caressed his face. Roderick closed his strong arms more tightly around her. She exhaled slowly.

"My family didn't give you the warmest welcome."

Roderick let out a hearty laugh. "Oh it was warm, all right," he said sarcastically without heat.

"That's what I mean. Jacob came on like Jackson through Vicksburg, Adam acted like the last stand of the Alamo, and Daddy—well he's been too quiet. Like the calm before the storm. I know my father and Jacob. I feel like they're up to something and I don't want our marriage to get caught up in it or be a casualty because of it."

Roderick lifted her chin to look into her eyes. "Your family is important to you and you love them. I respect that and I understand it. Family loyalty is a very important part of my life, too, but you're my family now, Jai. *We* are a family. You, our children, and me. I'll do whatever I have to do to keep us together as a family unit, even if that means making peace with your father and brothers. What I won't do is let anyone, not your family or mine, come between us. You're in my blood, Jai, just as I am in yours. I'm yours without question. Every fiber of my being is dedicated to you and making sure you're happy."

Roderick's mouth touched down on JaiHonnah's and covered hers. He stroked her hair, lacing his fingers through the thick, black, silky curls, pulling her deeper into the kiss. She opened to him, moving her body up higher on his.

"I love you so much it hurts," she said, trembling against his lips, tears rimming her eyes. "But I'm afraid…"

"Shhh," Roderick said, soothingly.

He rolled her onto her back and came up on top of her. He closed off her words and her fears with his kiss. Their tongues danced erotically together, giving rise to his nature. Her hardened nipples tortured his chest and he captured each of them as if sucking sweet nectar. JaiHonnah's moans and the gyrations of her hips against him caused him to shudder with sweet agony.

All he wanted to do was weld himself inside her again. To join himself to her, but he had to hold off his own desire. His breathing came back under his control. He cupped her butt and then slid out of sight beneath the silk comforter. Wrapped in the warmth between her thighs, Roderick worked his way slowly and painstakingly toward her sweet spot.

JaiHonnah wanted to scream out her pleasure when Roderick's velvety soft tongue captured her. The texture of his mustache shot her system up and over the edge, but Roderick held her hips in his massive hands. With her eyes tightly closed, she couldn't see what he was doing to her, only his touch, his deep groans, and the movement of the comforter gave any forewarning of what he would do next. Soon it didn't matter. The fire of her passion consumed her. Her heart was thumping against her chest, threatening to extinguish her every breath.

"Roderick," she moaned raggedly over and over again, as she reached another climax.

Slowly, Roderick eased himself to his knees, feathering his kisses and caresses over JaiHonnah's body. Her scent incensed him beyond consciousness and her desperate cries for him threatened to eclipse his ability to hold off his overwhelming desire to please her first. His fullness beat to another cadence and the tempo grew steadily. When he reached the hollow of her throat, her nails tore into his flesh.

"Roderick . . . please . . . I want you now," she moaned, as she pressed herself against him. "You're driving me crazy."

Still on his hands and knees hovering above her, Roderick's deep-throated, husky laugh came against her ear. "Now you have some clue of what you do to me. I can't get enough of you."

JaiHonnah captured his shaft and exercised it.

"Where are you—" was all he was able to say before her mouth encased him. She deftly controlled him, demanding his flesh burn in her hot, wet mouth. Roderick sucked in ragged breaths through gritted teeth. His deep groans caught in his throat, as she played her tongue against, around, and over him. A shudder raced up his spine.

"Jai... no more . . . please . . . I can't . . . hold off any longer," he said, quickly finding her mouth and her wicked tongue that threatened to be his undoing.

Roderick fixed his position and braced himself on his arms. Slowly, but methodically, he began thrusting as JaiHonnah thrust against him. She took all of him in her tight, wet, muscular sheath. He could no longer hold back. To even try would mean certain madness. JaiHonnah milked him for all he had. They reached nirvana simultaneously and drifted into euphoria.

"Now you have some clue of what I feel," JaiHonnah whispered devilishly, breathlessly against his ear.

"*Touché*, Mrs. Baylor," Roderick laughed raggedly. "*Touché*."

Chapter Three

A MONTH LATER, AFTER THE WEDDING and honeymoon, the ecstasy had only gotten better. Roderick put down the reports he was reading. He tried for hours to refocus his thoughts and he was getting nowhere fast. He sat in his office with his feet up on his desk and his hands laced behind his head, savoring the vision in his head of his and JaiHonnah's lovemaking that morning. Leaving his bed upstairs in the penthouse condo, with JaiHonnah still in it—warm, sleepy, and soft—was the hardest thing he had to do each day. Too many days, lured by that vision, he would cut a meeting short and climb the steps from his business office to the residential level of their home to find her. While the girls were at school and the boys took an unscheduled nap, he and JaiHonnah would reach the passageway to total fulfillment.

The Washington, DC, skyline held no interest for him. Nor did the sight of his yacht, *The Navajo Princess*, docked behind his home/office/warehouse complex.

Roderick stretched his body and felt the shudder that had led him upstairs to their sanctuary. His nature was rapidly rising. Then he noticed his office door slide open slowly and JaiHonnah's devilish grin peeking in, warming him. He grinned at her in a like fashion.

"Yes, Mrs. Baylor, was there something you wanted?" he asked with a gleam in his eyes and a grin curling his mouth.

JaiHonnah stepped inside the door and closed it behind her back. Roderick heard the click of the lock falling into place. She eyed his out-stretched body so lasciviously from head to toe that his groin tightened and swelled against his slacks even more.

"Uh, yes, Mr. Baylor," she cooed, seductively moving languidly toward him and then around his desk. "There is something I want." JaiHonnah ran a lazy finger up his leg, inside his thigh and caressed his thickness through his slacks. While looking him in the eye, she slowly pulled his zipper down and reached inside, exposing him. Climbing onto his lap, facing him, she inserted him inside her slowly and steadily, rocking back and forth as if on a hobby horse.

Roderick's heart raced with the anticipation and anxiety caused by his wife's sexy seduction. The fact that she was not wearing panties under her wide skirt caused his manhood to twitch and enlarge. He grinned at her, as she lowered her head and lightly touched down on his lips, outlining his mouth with her tongue.

"I was not finished with you this morning, Mr. Baylor," she said through soft, short breaths against his lips, as she rocked her hips steadily, tightening and releasing her inner muscles around him.

"Uh, Reise and Rodney seemed to think their needs were greater than ours at that moment," he said, breathing raggedly.

"You'll have to speak with our sons about that during your early morning, male-bonding sessions. You three men seem to have a lot to talk about."

"Speak? Mrs. Baylor, if I'm not speechless when you finish mesmerizing me, you have me babbling like an idiot every morning. Reise and Rodney are a little too young to understand their father isn't sane with their mother anywhere in the vicinity. I don't think our sons would understand a word I was trying to say."

"What? The devastatingly handsome, very articulate, and deftly creative, Rock of Gibraltar, Mr. John Roderick Baylor, is claiming he can't talk and think at the same time?"

"You clearly understand my dilemma and my disability, Mrs. Baylor, and, if you keep up this sweet torture, I'll demonstrate the point to you momentarily. You have a debilitating effect on me. I haven't accomplished a thing all day."

"Then while you're still coherent," she suckled his lips, "and I have your full attention," she outlined his mouth with her tongue, "I thought I'd mention we're having guests for dinner tonight." She rocked a little more forcefully. "Vivian and Chuck are back in town," she said through deep breaths in his ear, as she held his hands together behind his head and continued to coax his nature from his sacks. "They'll be here at eight. Until then I thought I'd make something to eat," she lathed his neck with her tongue, "since Mrs. Betterman just took the boys out for a long, long stroll along the riverfront. Then I thought I'd take a long, long leisurely soak before I started to prepare dinner. Is there anything I can do for you, Mr. Baylor, while I have this free time on my hands?" she cooed.

The pressure she exerted on his libido built to capacity. Roderick's breath came in quick pants until his eyes slammed shut, his face contorted in painful ecstasy, and his body convulsed. He sucked in air through clinched teeth, trying to contain his thundering heartbeat.

JaiHonnah slowly removed herself from Roderick's lap and moved toward the door, suggestively swaying her hips. She winked at Roderick over her shoulder. "If you want to continue this conversation, Mr. Baylor, you know where I'll be." Eyeing him sensuously, she unlocked the door and slipped out.

Perspiration dampened Roderick's shirt, causing it to cling to his body. He was speechless. His wife's seduction of him was complete and utterly beguiling. Finally, his faculties began to return. He pushed a button on his intercom console.

"Yes, Mr. Baylor?" his assistant answered.

"What's on my schedule this afternoon?" he asked, clearing his throat.

"Well, you have three meetings scheduled, one with—"

"Reschedule them all. I'm going to lunch."

His secretary giggled. *"Again?"*

"Yes, again," he said, stifling his own amusement as he rose from his chair.

Roderick repositioned himself and zipped his pants. He was unbuttoning his shirt as he took the steps from his office two at a time to their penthouse. He left a trail of clothes as he headed toward the sound of the bubbling Jacuzzi.

Later that evening, as Roderick sat at the kitchen table feeding Reise and Rodney, while helping Shelley and Shelby complete their homework, JaiHonnah put the finishing touches on a Café-au-Lait cheesecake. The doorbell rang and JaiHonnah went to the security screen on the wall and flipped it on.

"Kelley." She smiled broadly, as she pushed the buzzer opening the door.

Shortly, Kelley Baylor, Roderick's sister, came up in the elevator that opened to the penthouse condo. Shelley and Shelby enthusiastically greeted their aunt with hugs and kisses.

"Why didn't you just use your key, Kelley?" JaiHonnah asked, as she hugged her. "You didn't have to ring us."

"With you newlyweds, I thought I'd better let someone know I was coming." She knowingly grinned. "It's nice to see you two come up for air every once in a while. I just stopped by to deliver these papers. Mmmm, something smells delicious," she said, kissing Roderick on the top of his head and then moving to hug and kiss her nephews.

Roderick grinned and winked at JaiHonnah. "You caught us at an off moment," he said with a gleam in his eyes.

"I should say so. How many more meetings are you going to postpone with me, little brother? Perhaps I should try again next year," she teased.

Roderick rolled his eyes upward. "Ah," he exhaled, "I'm sorry, Kelley, I completely forgot."

Kelley giggled. "I should say you did."

"Why don't you stay for dinner? Vivian and Chuck are coming over at about eight o'clock," JaiHonnah said.

"Sure, I'd love to, if it wouldn't be an imposition."

"No imposition. We've made enough to feed a small army. Plus it will give you time to spend with your nephews and nieces, right guys?" Roderick asked.

The girls cheered and clapped. It warmed Kelley to see the happy family gathered together, doing what all families should do—spend quality time together. Roderick and JaiHonnah looked blissfully happy, as well they should. Roderick's recent uncharacteristic behavior, of spending many more hours at home with JaiHonnah than at work, was the source of much office gossip

Kelley heard. It was all good natured and much of it funny. The whole staff was taking bets on how soon another Baylor would be born.

Roderick and JaiHonnah's happy life paled her life by comparison, thought Kelley. That was true of her other brothers, sister, and their spouses. Of her four siblings, she was the only one unmarried and childless. The happiness her brothers, sister, brother-in-law and sisters-in-law shared put a spotlight on her sometimes lonely forty years of life. She dated heavily and even fancied herself infatuated with some of the men she knew, but no one gave her much more than an occasional night of hot passion. Nothing stirred her interest enough to make a concerted effort to see any of them for more than one season of the year—that is until Jake Hawkins, JaiHonnah's father, happened on the scene.

Now there was a man for *all* seasons, she thought. From the moment he marched into her business office behind two behemoths dressed in fancy Texas garb, he was the most exquisite specimen of male this side of heaven she had ever seen. His Texas Stetson barely made it under the overhang of the front door. She had to take a quick breath because this man had to be Billy Dee Williams' better-looking brother, she thought. His boldness and blatant masculinity intrigued her and caused her to sweat. She remained cool to him though. She sensed Jake Hawkins had his pick of women anywhere and anytime he chose. She had no intention of becoming another in his long line of castoffs. Plus, theoretically, Jake Hawkins' conglomerate, BlackHawk International, and Roderick's company, Baylor Design and Development, were still fierce competitors in the construction industry despite Roderick's and JaiHonnah's marriage and despite the fact Roderick held a seat on Jake's board of directors. Jake's business, however, was far larger and more diverse than Baylor Design. The BlackHawk companies had fingers in many pies, so to speak, and in some critical areas, he owned a substantial part of the known universe. Letting herself succumb to Jake's many charms might compromise Baylor Industries, the division she headed, or even JR Baylor, Limited, the parent corporation. Where Jake Hawkins was concerned, she had to keep her head and her distance. His reputation, both public and private, labeled him as no ordinary man.

Kelley helped Roderick and the girls bathe the boys, read several stories to them, and put them to bed. She moved on to help JaiHonnah set the dinner table. As they worked, she and JaiHonnah talked and laughed about ordinary things. The comradery between them was always fun.

Obviously, Roderick was a very good husband. Kelley noticed it by the blush that warmed JaiHonnah's beautiful face whenever she mentioned his name. It was that glow Kelley longed for in her own life.

When the doorbell rang, "I'll get it," Roderick said. "It must be Vivian and Chuck." He looked at his watch. "They're early." Roderick flipped on the security monitor and his eyes narrowed. "Uh, I'll buzz you in," he said drolly. "Take the elevator to the third floor."

Something about Jake Hawkins' presence made people stop in their tracks. Roderick hadn't felt the sensation with anyone other than his own father, John Baylor. Jake cut a wide, tall, and broad trail when he entered a room. Roderick stood stiffly with feet apart, back straight, head up, and arms folded across his chest. He didn't know what to make of his father-in-law's unannounced visit. His daughters, however, were elated and undaunted by Jake's presence. They ran and jumped into his arms, kissing him the same way they did their father. Roderick noticed how Jake lit up, receiving the warmth and kisses. It was odd thinking of Jake Hawkins as a man who loved children—a twenty-first century grandfather.

This captain of industry, with the Midas touch, had done it all in his life and amassed a fortune. His company was high on the Fortune 500 and still climbing, but here he was reveling in Shelley's and Shelby's embraces as if there was nothing more important in the world to do.

"Daddy!" JaiHonnah squealed when she saw her father enter the open floor plan living quarters. "What a surprise."

Kelley's brows narrowed and she and her brother briefly glimpsed each other.

"How you doin', dahlin'?" Jake grinned, putting the twins on the floor and enveloping JaiHonnah tightly.

"What brings you to Washington?" she asked, smiling.

"Had a little business to do with my senators and congressmen. Thought I'd just stop in and say hello while I was here. Hope I'm not intruding."

JaiHonnah glimpsed Roderick's imperious expression and he noticed. Jake released JaiHonnah and faced Roderick. Their stare lasted many uncomfortable moments before they almost simultaneously extended a hand to each other.

"You been taking care of my JaiHawk?" Jake asked, firmly shaking Roderick's hand.

"Did you think I wouldn't take care of my wife?" Roderick asked without expression.

Then Jake's gaze landed on Kelley Baylor and stayed while he spoke. "You youngsters don't always know what a real woman needs. Don't always take the time to make sure she's satisfied, fulfilled emotionally, and happy," he said, still eyeing Kelley. He released Roderick's hand and sauntered slowly, but deliberately toward Kelley. "A woman is like a fine wine. You have to savor the flavor. Roll it around on your pallet to experience the years a great vintage needs to ripen." He raised Kelley's hand to his lips, his creamy, southern drawl whispering through his words. "Miz. Baylor," he acknowledged her, his eyes smoldered with heat, as his lips touched down on the back of her hand. "Yes, a fine wine, like a fine woman, ripens and improves with age. Shouldn't leave those grapes on the vine too long though. Not properly handled, tended to with care, a fine wine can turn to vinegar, am I right, Miz. Baylor?"

"You're obviously a connoisseur, Mr. Hawkins. However, bourbon, straight, fits my pallet. Wine is for those who can't do any better, can't handle the *hard* stuff. Now, take Kentucky Bourbon, for example. Now that puts air in your whistle. Holds your interests longer. When you've had a good shot of a Kentucky

Gentleman, you know you've been had," she said smugly with a half-cocked eyebrow.

Roderick and JaiHonnah gave each other a furtive sideways glance. They could feel the heat and knew there had to be a fire smoldering.

"Uh, could I offer either of you a drink?" Roderick asked to break the tension.

"Bourbon for me and the lady," Jake said, not taking his eyes from Kelley. "Straight," he added, "no chaser."

Roderick poured the drinks and handed them to Jake and Kelley.

"Uh, look, Hawkins, we're having some people over for dinner," Roderick said. "If you have nothing else planned, Jai and I would...well, the boys are already asleep, but I thought, since you haven't seen them in a while, you might want to spend some time with them. You're welcomed to stay and join us for dinner."

JaiHonnah's heart leaped for joy when Roderick spontaneously invited her father to have dinner with them and spend some time with their sons, Jake's grandsons. He was the only grandparent the boys and Roderick's twin girls had. She stood by Roderick's side and put her arms around his waist, looking up at him with pride in her expression.

Jake was surprised by, but very pleased with, the sincerity of Roderick's offer. His tone made him feel truly welcomed into his new son-in-law's home. Looking at the glow on his daughter's face also pleased him. He had never seen that glow on her face when she was married to Calvin Chapman.

"Thanks, I'd like that. Oh, yes, I almost forgot," Jake said, reaching into his inside pocket. "I bought you two a little wedding gift." He handed the envelope to Roderick.

Roderick opened it and unfolded the deed to a one-hundred ninety-acre estate in Charles County, Maryland. The deed was already in his and JaiHonnah's names and the receipt read: PAID IN FULL. Two sets of keys were also in the envelope.

Roderick's jaw tightened. "Thanks, but we can't accept this," he said, handing the papers back to Jake.

"Well, I know it's not a big place. Kinda small for my taste, but I thought it might make a nice home for JaiHawk's stallions. Can't keep horses like Hawk and Knight Hawk in the city."

"*Hawk and Knight Hawk?*" JaiHonnah squealed. "You're giving them to me?"

Jake laughed at her exuberance. "Had them and a few of their buddies and lady friends delivered today. Best twelve of the herd you brought down from the hills the day Baylor showed up. Got some nice brood mares in the lot. Hawk's been busy since your wedding and so has Knight Hawk. Look to see about six foals come spring."

JaiHonnah could barely contain herself until she felt Roderick's stiffened stance. She reined in her excitement.

"Uh, Daddy, this was very thoughtful of you, but Roderick's right. It's too much. You could give us some Tupperware or something." She smiled and kissed him on the cheek.

"Well, think it over, Baylor. The horses are being taken care of. If you don't want to live there, you can use the place to stable the horses. At least Jai, Shelley and Shelby would have somewhere to ride occasionally. I imagine Jai will want Rodney and Reise to learn to ride too."

Roderick could feel the excitement in his wife's demeanor. "I'll take it into consideration," he said.

Chuck and Vivian Alexander Montgomery arrived for dinner and the group of six settled into an evening of tense fun and frivolity. The discussions ran the gambit, but never touched on business. Everyone just seemed to want to enjoy the evening and they worked hard at it.

Chuck pushed his plate away from him. "That's it. I can't eat another morsel." He sighed.

"Neither can I, JaiHawk. You set a great feedbag," Jake said, rubbing his stomach.

"Oh, I didn't do the cooking," she admitted with a smile. "Roderick's the magic chef in this household. I'm the sous chef."

"Not bad, JRock," Vivian said, smiling.

"You ought to be around when he's really trying," Kelley said, laughing. "He should teach B. Smith how to burn."

"So you did this, JRock?" Chuck asked. "Maybe I should have married you instead of Vivian. Boiling water makes her nervous." He laughed.

Vivian pursed her lips. "Uh, honey, you didn't marry me for my culinary skills, did you?"

Everyone laughed and so did Chuck. "You're right, Viv. Your judicial deliberations in the kitchen did not weigh on my long wait and decision to let you make an honest man of me," he said, sealing the statement with a kiss on her lips.

"When are the hearings starting on your nomination for the Circuit Court of Appeals judgeship, Viv?" Kelley asked.

Vivian turned her glance toward Jake with a devilish, winged eyebrow. "Uh, when are they starting, Jake?" she questioned.

Jake felt the pressure of her gaze and covered his face briefly with one hand. "Uh, hearing? Uh, well uh, I understand it's scheduled for Thursday morning. Uh, Senator Billings mentioned it in passing at lunch today."

Everyone at the table noticed the cat-and-mouse game being played out between Vivian and Jake, with Jake playing the role of the mouse.

"Vivian, did my father have something to do with your name being submitted to the Congress by the President?"

"Uh, I couldn't swear on my oath that Jake Hawkins' fine finger of fate wasn't somewhere in there. Chuck and I ran into Adam in South Africa at an American Embassy dinner honoring businessmen and businesswomen who are investing in the country. The former President of South Africa made a point of telling me my assistance with bringing about more American investment and trade would be sorely missed after I was robed. Your brother wasn't a bit surprised, it seemed. In fact, to him, it was a *fete accompli*."

Roderick's radar went up, as did JaiHonnah's, but hers for an entirely different reason. Roderick wondered if Adam was in South Africa, then he might have stumbled on to certain business information Roderick did not want made public. Perhaps Jake's impromptu visit tonight included certain other hidden agendas, he thought. Roderick realized his attention to his businesses had suffered since the wedding, but he intended to rectify the problem first thing Monday morning.

"Does this mean you'll have to leave your law firm, Vivian?" Kelley asked.

"Not only that, but also sever certain business dealings or put them in a blind trust," she said, eyeing Jake. "The Senate Ethics Committee is very strict about what investments a judicial candidate can hold. There can't even be the appearance of impropriety in any aspect of my dealings. Of course, if I'm appointed to the federal bench, I am restricted from hearing any case my firm is involved in and certainly not any case I argued at the lower court level—isn't that right, Jake?" Jake shifted uncomfortably in his seat, but Vivian continued without awaiting his response. "Every contact I make with a former client would have to have a record made of not only the contact, but also the nature of the conversation. Nothing will be private anymore, if my nomination is confirmed."

"No doubt it will be," Roderick said, knowingly eyeing Jake. Vivian was his legal counsel for many years and they held certain businesses in common.

JaiHonnah silently echoed Roderick's thoughts. Her father loved Vivian like a daughter since she and Vivian were college roommates at Spelman. Jake loved to play chess with Vivian, and JaiHonnah was sure they probably still had a game underway. She wondered, not for the first time, what her father was up to. There was definitely something afoot.

Roderick rose early the next morning and started the coffee before anyone else was awake. He sat alone in the kitchen area and thought about the previous evening. It did go well, he thought. He and Jake were not at each other's throats, although it was clear to Roderick Jake made tactical moves to supplant Vivian as his legal adviser. Although everything that transpired between him and Vivian came under the heading of privileged information, the absence of her intuition, sound judgment, and legal skills would be sorely missed. He would have to use one of her other law firm partners to handle his affairs.

Under ordinary circumstances, it would not present a problem, but he and Vivian won many wars together, some of them against Jake Hawkins or some of his cronies. He sensed a new day was dawning and he would have to be ready to meet the challenge. He hoped he wasn't starting this challenge too late. Still, that was nothing new. He faced challenges throughout his life. His early childhood was not Disney World inspired.

The youngest son of five children, his parents sometimes worked two, full-time jobs each to make ends meet, yet there was often more month left over after the money ran out. He never went to bed hungry, but extras were few and far between.

He remembered what happened on the night he took JaiHonnah to his old neighborhood in advance of his plan to demolish the old community. He wanted her to get a feel for what he was trying to accomplish with the construction of Baylor Plaza Park. The new, planned community was to be a tribute he would build in honor of his parents and those other men and women from his childhood community who tried to make life better in his decaying neighborhood.

The graffiti-stained, run-down, and poorly-lit shopping center in the heart of his old neighborhood looked like the remnants of a war zone.

Wesley Greenfield, aka Ice, was still his best friend. Roderick hoped to convince him to reopen the shop, but visions of Wesley's father's murder locking up one night still shocked the community.

Ice was running a community center now instead of opening the shop in the dying shopping center.

"Jai, I wanted you to see this place. Partly because I wanted you to see who I am and where I came from, but also because I want you to know what you're up against. This is not Fairfax County, Virginia. It's a tough neighborhood and the people in it aren't the country club type. You have your work cut out for you. I don't want this to fail like so many other model cities projects have. It's too important to me and the people, like my parents, Rosalyn, Ice, Tavon, Peckhead and others who chose to stick it out under some of the worst conditions imaginable." He had stopped talking and looked around. *"Something has got to turn this community around. Government can't, won't, and shouldn't do it alone. It's a cliché, but it's true. It's going to take everyone pulling together to make this work. It all starts with you and your magic-making architectural brain, Mrs. Chapman."* He had kissed her on the forehead, put his arm around her shoulders and walked toward his car, which had some young thugs on bicycles standing guard over it. This time his car was untouched.

As he sat drinking his coffee, he remembered how JaiHonnah bought into his dream for the revival of his old neighborhood.

Now, they were full steam ahead and making good progress on the Baylor Plaza Park project. The project, headed by his friend and Project Manager, Wesley Greenfield, aka, Ice, wasn't as large as the seventeen-hundred-acre Rock Creek Park in Northwest, Washington, DC, but much larger than the forty-two-acre Fort DuPont Park in Southeast, DC. Baylor Plaza Park was shaping up to be a model, one-of-a-kind community that appealed to all income and social levels. It was conceded that JaiHonnah's plan of a woodland village concept was nothing less than brilliant. He was enormously proud of her.

Chapter Four

AS RODERICK PERUSED THE MORNING NEWSPAPER, an article caught his eye.

Loan for the District of Columbia a No Go, the caption read. *The DC financial Control Board Chairman, said yesterday, before a congressional oversight panel, chaired by Congressman Thomas of Texas, the city will not be permitted to borrow hundreds of millions of dollars to pay off its accumulating budget deficit…'The Mayor must do more to control spending' said the Congressman…. The Mayor argued the city needs six hundred million to cover its budget deficits, to reform its management systems, and revamp city roads and other city capital improvement projects, like the model cities project being constructed at Baylor Plaza Park... New York financial officials stated the city has not done enough to control spending... The rush by the city to fund capital improvement projects has recently come under fire. Sources say such projects, albethey needed, should not be made a priority. Rather, the administration's close and long-held ties with the business community, including the city-based Baylor Design and Development Company, is said to be at the center of the drive... Questions have been raised by the Congressional Oversight Committee about the number of projects certain developers are able to whisk through the DC governments offices without close scrutiny. Chairman Thomas vowed to begin an investigation into what he termed 'the incestuous relationship' between the administration and certain highly visible and well-connected developers...*

Roderick put down the newspaper. The inference in the article was that somehow *he* was receiving preferential treatment by the local government for his projects. Of course, nothing could be further from the truth. He simply had a competent staff of engineers, accountants, and planners who knew their jobs and how to get things done. He shook his head in frustration.

Well, he thought, if the good and honorable Congressman from the great State of Texas wanted to investigate his dealings with the city, let him! He had nothing to hide.

Roderick steepled his hands as something began to dawn on him. Congressman Thomas was from the southwestern part of Texas—Hawkins' district. He wondered whether Jake was wielding his considerable influence and clout where the Oversight Committee was concerned. It wasn't too farfetched to be a consideration. Jake did that before, he knew. He had studied Jake Hawkins' moves when he got the scent of something Jake was after. He would use anything and anyone to succeed.

Jake admitted, during dinner the previous night, he met with the congressman and this tactical move, tying up the city's ability to borrow money to fund city capital improvement projects, had, in Roderick's view, a giant Hawkins brand on it. "Uh-huh," he thought aloud. "Time to move a chess piece into place to block Hawkins." Roderick picked up the telephone and dialed a number.

"Hello," a weary voice answered.

"I want you to free up six hundred million," he said.

"*Dollars?*" the voice croaked back.

"Yes, American money."

"JRock, what is it for? I mean, you're facing some grave financial problems—"

"Just do it, China."

Frustrated, China McAllister, his Chief Financial Officer, exhaled. "Yes, sir."

When Roderick hung up, his thoughts turned to JaiHonnah. She seemed so pleased that her father gave her his prize-winning stallions. He recalled the excitement in her eyes when she rode like the wind. His daughters were taking riding lessons now and were becoming very good at it, too. Roderick loved to see JaiHonnah and his twins dressed in their riding habits. Perhaps the idea of keeping the horses at the Charles County estate wouldn't be such a bad idea, he thought. He knew it would make JaiHonnah very happy. He loved her so much he was willing to put his prideful position aside for JaiHonnah's pleasure. Suddenly, he needed to be close to her.

Roderick slipped back into bed and spooned JaiHonnah, who was lying on her side. He kissed her back and her neck and slid his hand around her waist.

"Good morning," he groaned into her ear.

JaiHonnah found his hand and kissed his palm, placing it on her breast.

"Good morning," she said, wiggling closer to him. She felt the hard ridge of his nature pressing against her back, as he massaged her breast. "You're up early this morning, I see."

Roderick turned JaiHonnah onto her back, partially resting his weight on the side of her. He slipped his hand between her thighs and met the heat and moisture he craved.

"Seems that I'm not the only one up early this morning," he groaned in her ear. She was warm and wet. Ready to receive him.

JaiHonnah giggled and lifted her hips, welcoming him. The ecstasy began.

Jake Hawkins braced himself again, his manly canon's rapid discharge for what seemed like an eternity and then he slumped, sweating profusely. His heart had not beaten that hard in too many years. He was wiped out, feeling as if he had just run in the Olympic Games—and won the gold. A woman like Kelley Baylor was sure to have been with other men, he knew, but what he didn't know was whether any of them survived the experience. She rocked his world from the moment he brought her home to her place from dinner with her brother and Jai. He reached for the flame in his life before, but this woman taught him what hot really meant.

Kelley's mind was completely blown. She had to check to see whether her body returned from whatever universe Jake Hawkins had sent it. She braced herself for his large phallus, but not for the thunderous emotions he drew from her. Throughout the night, the rushes she felt defied description and it was a good thing, too. She couldn't be coherent even if she tried to talk. The last intelligible and lucid words she remembered saying to Jake were, "Would you like to come in for a nightcap?" After that, everything else was a series of grunts, groans, hallelujahs and yippee kayos. She wondered vaguely whether his chauffeur was still sitting outside of her townhouse with the motor running. Strange thing to think about now in the afterglow with her still quaking from the last erotic encounter. She tried to move, but found that impossible. Jake was still lying on top of her.

"Woman, whatever you do, please don't move a muscle doing it," Jake complained.

"I don't have a muscle left to move," she moaned seriously.

Jake raised his head and looked into her eyes. He cocked his eyebrow and a grin rimmed his lips.

"Want to try working on that last muscle again?"

Kelley's pursed lips softened into a devilish grin.

"All right, family, we're going on a little excursion today," Roderick announced while briskly rubbing his hands together.

JaiHonnah looked quizzically over her shoulder at him, as she stored the milk and juice in the refrigerator. He said nothing about an outing earlier. She wondered what he was up to; he was becoming as mercurial as her father.

Shelley and Shelby quickly finished putting the breakfast dishes in the dishwasher and scampered away to get their brothers' jackets and hats. Within a few minutes they were all seated in the family SUV and tooling down the highway. They were gleeful all the way, as Roderick drove south of Washington for more than one hour. Once they entered Charles County, Roderick pulled onto a private road that led to the property Jake had gifted to them. As the narrow, winding road proceeded through the beautiful fall-dressed forested area, a spectacular mansion loomed before them. He heard JaiHonnah and his daughters catch their breaths, as he pulled into the circular driveway. The place was breathtakingly beautiful and mammoth, he silently admitted. Well-landscaped, waterfront property with an abundance of wildlife in clear view. Deer ambled lazily around the acreage. Birds chirped gaily in the trees, squirrels hopped along the grounds. There was an absolute quiet and pastoral, peaceful feel to the property.

Peace.

Roderick carried Reise and JaiHonnah carried Rodney, as they began to explore, with Shelley and Shelby darting here and there.

They entered the three-story mansion and their eyes were drawn immediately to the wide-open expanse and sweeping views of the Wicomico River at the back of the property. The dramatic sunken living room's cathedral, ceiling-high windows and doors had a panoramic view. They walked out onto a deck via two sets of doors and the Wicomico River and Charleston Creek surrounded them on two sides. Ducks and geese drifted lazily on the water. A two-hundred-foot pier stretched out into Charleston Creek.

Back inside, the open and spacious, formal dining hall overlooked one of the living spaces, leading to a screened-in porch via two sets of doors. The kitchen was a little dated, the appliances weren't the most modern or energy efficient, but the room was immense with solid oak cabinets on each wall space. A nook with stained chair-rail and crown molding as well as a walk-in pantry, a laundry room, a mudroom, and a powder room expanded the charm of the surroundings, but the rest of the rooms made up for those shortcomings.

A library, salon, and music/media rooms made up the additional rooms on the first floor. Through another hallway was a door that led to a four-car garage. Above it were servant's quarters; two, two-bedroom fully-equipped apartments.

Six bedroom suites were on one side of the mansion separate from the massive master bedroom suite and allowing the maximum privacy. The master bedroom suite took up one half of the mansion's upper floor with a private deck off the back. Walk-around closets were perfectly designed. The master bath had a dated, massive, whirlpool tub with gold-plated hardware fixtures. An office space and a separate sitting room overlooked the south side of the property.

The walkout basement had a terrific recreation room with chair rail, a kitchenette and a wet bar with brass sink. Again, the space was in desperate need of revitalization. The same expansive view of the river could be seen through the French doors. Doors from the recreation room led to a patio, a full bath with shower, and two more bedroom suites. Exiting the mansion through the basement's French doors, they walked toward a corral outside the largest barn, and the horse stalls attached to a large, three-story bunkhouse. Two men came out of the stalls and waved.

"You must be Ms. JaiHawk," one of the men said with a Texas-sized smile, extending his hand.

"JaiHonnah Hawkins Baylor and this is my husband, Roderick Baylor," she said to the men, extending her hand. "JaiHawk is my nickname, but how'd you know?"

"Hawk started kicking up a ruckus. Figured he must have known you were here."

Just then, a third man led Hawk out of the covered stalls. The horse pranced in place and broke for the fence toward JaiHonnah, stopping just short. She handed Rodney to Roderick and climbed the corral fence to greet the horse. She stroked him and climbed aboard his bare back, riding him around the corral.

Roderick mentally weighed all of the arguments against accepting Jake Hawkins' gift, but the look of pure country on JaiHonnah's face sealed the deal. She was born and raised on a ranch in Hawkins' country. Farming, cattle, and horses were in her blood. She may have been well schooled around the world, having won beauty pageants, but she still had hayseed in her hair.

She was magnificent, as she rode. It was clear to him she and Hawk belonged together. Horse and rider would have jumped the fence at the slightest provocation and been off racing around the hundred and ninety acres, he thought. His daughters, no doubt, would have been riding with her and probably his sons, too, whose eyes widened at the sight of the steed. Mentally, he estimated the market price of the property in its current condition. He would have to commit considerable resources to the remodel and upgrades he noted, but it was a small price to pay for his wife and children's happiness.

JaiHonnah tried to stifle her enthusiasm, but she could feel the blush coloring her face. She didn't look into Roderick's eyes when she dismounted Hawk. She climbed over the corral fence and took Reise from Roderick's arms. They started walking back toward the mansion quietly. JaiHonnah was worrying her bottom lip. She only glanced over her shoulder twice at Hawk.

"Lousy place, wouldn't you say, Jai?" Roderick asked, as they walked. "A lot of renovations on the surface before taking out walls. Very expensive to upgrade all of the utilities."

"Terrible. Right, girls?" JaiHonnah asked.

The twins were silent and then stopped and looked up at JaiHonnah and Roderick.

"Why can't we live here, Daddy?" Shelby asked.

"Can't," Roderick said with a shrug.

Shelley knitted her brow and cocked her head to one side. "Why not, Daddy?"

"It doesn't have an indoor/outdoor swimming pool," he said nonchalantly.

"So build one, Daddy," Shelley whined. "We're a builder, right?"

"Well, I guess we could do that, but I'd need a lot of help."

"We'll all help you, Daddy," Shelby said seriously.

Roderick looked at JaiHonnah's pained expression and a grin curled his lips. "Only if Jai tells us where to put it," he said, smiling.

"Yes!" JaiHonnah said loudly, jerking the air with one fist.

From that moment, Roderick's life wasn't his own. JaiHonnah was in seventh heaven, redesigning the mansion's interior and re-landscaping the grounds to accommodate the indoor/outdoor pool, a tennis court, a basketball court, and designing a larger barn to hold the horses and other animals she and his girls planned to have. She bought vacant land on both sides of their property to expand the estate into more of a ranch. She had his construction crews working overtime and sometimes double time to complete the renovations. When she was finished, the mansion alone had doubled in value. Just before Christmas, they moved into their new home and named the estate-cum-ranch Deer Haven.

Chapter Five

CHINA MCALLISTER, A BLOND, BLUE-EYED, bronze beauty came straight to the point. "Someone's gradually buying up Baylor Industry stock and selling short."

Roderick raised his head and looked at her. "What's the stock worth now?"

"Earnings or net worth?"

"Both."

"Over the past year, since you went public, the minority stock is worth about," she named a figure. "Net worth?" she said, shrugging. Your earning potential has been on the decline since September."

"What does this mean, Roderick?" Kelley asked.

"We don't have enough of a demand for our services, it seems. The building industry, just like any other industry, goes through a cyclical pattern. At the moment we're on the decline."

"Also someone is making sure you don't come up again, JRock," Bill Chandler, a founding partner with Vivian's law firm, added. "The problems you're facing wouldn't be half as serious if someone wasn't selling your stock short."

"Tell me something I don't already know, Bill," Roderick said behind steepled fingers. "Rothman Childs' bank turned down my request to borrow what I need to finance a stock buyback. That leaves me more than a little short, if I can't find another bank." He wasn't particularly concerned. His friend and venture capitalist, Nicholas Collins, told him he always had access to funds through Nick's financial institution.

"Yes, it does," China added.

"JRock, you can, of course, start selling off parts of Baylor Industries. You bought the brick, block, and masonry company, the lumber yard, and the plumbing supply store several years ago. You could sell them now and maybe make a profit. We could use subcontractors instead of our own people to complete work on the demolition and restructuring of the Olympic sites."

Roderick stood from his reflective position and slowly paced with his hands dug down in his pockets. "The market would go nuts if Baylor Industries started divesting. It would be a sure signal we're in trouble. Then I'd have to fend off more hostile takeover attempts."

"The existing stock would drop faster than a whore's panties in the Navy Yard," Bill agreed.

"Then what do you want to do, JRock?" Kelley asked.

"I'm going to have to arrange for another loan, probably for another half billion from Nicholas Collins."

"That's going to give you the funds you need to buy out the minority stockholders," China agreed.

"Yes, but it also does something else. In order to do this, I'm going to have to call a meeting of the board of directors. Then I can call for a stockholders' meeting and whoever is doing this will have to show his or her hand."

"Sounds like a good strategy to me, JRock, but I'm primarily a sports and entertainment law attorney," Bill said. "You need someone working with you who understand securities law like Vivian does. When Vivian left the firm to accept the judgeship, I and the other founders started looking for two or three new senior partners to replace what she did alone. We're bringing in a top gun from New York as a full senior partner next week. I'll set up a meeting for you and give you a call."

"Thanks, Bill. In the meantime, I'll work on getting that loan. Kelley, I'm going to need a new prospectus from you. China, work on an updated profitability statement."

"Looks like another long weekend," China groaned. "JRock, you're ruining my social life. Since we've been working on this problem, I haven't had a free night in months." She looked at her watch. "And it looks like I've blown another date, too."

"Sorry, people," Roderick said. "It's not over 'til the buzzer sounds."

Everyone, but Kelley and Ice aka Wesley Greenfield, his childhood friend, rose to leave. Roderick shook everyone's hand and walked them out to the office door. When he returned, Ice looked up at him. He stood and angled a hip on the edge of the oak conference table. They exchanged a brother's handshake.

"JRock, I wish I knew how to help you with this. Seems like a shell game to me: Now you see it, then you don't."

"It can be that way, Ice. You've got to keep your eye on the rock and I haven't been doing that lately. Someone is dunking on me and I didn't see it coming."

"Well, my brother," Ice said, "If you can think of anything I can do, just let me know."

"Thanks, Ice. Keep your eyes peeled for what's going on at Baylor Plaza Park. Somehow, I don't think all the problems we've been having out at the site are purely coincidental."

"You got it, my man, and by the way, tell that fine foxy mama of yours, JaiHonnah, that the Iceman do cometh," he said, grinning.

"You tryin' to beat my time with my lady?" Roderick asked quizzically.

"Ha! Not with Roz around. I've got my own fox at home."

"*Whew!* That's good to hear. I haven't been able to spend much time with my family. I thought maybe she was ready to trade me in on a new model."

"Brotherman, don't be trippin'. Ain't no business that important with a woman like Jai waiting for you at home."

"I heard that."

"I'm outta here. See you, Kelley."

"Night, Ice," Kelley said drolly.

Ice left and Roderick noticed Kelley's reflective mood. He checked his watch and groaned. Another missed dinner with his children and wife, but Kelley seemed to be worried about something. He sat on the end of the conference table near her.

"What's up, Kelley? You've been chewing on something for weeks."

Kelley raised her eyes to Roderick and then stood. She paced with her hands on her hips. Then she abruptly turned and faced her brother.

"I have sinned!" she spat.

Roderick's head jerked back. He folded his arms across his chest. "You telling me you need to find religion or something, sister woman?" he teased.

"JRock, this is no laughing matter. I have sinned! I've been dancing with the devil in the pale moonlight and sleeping with the enemy! I let that devil man sweet talk me right out of my thong and probably caused you to lose your company!"

"Kelley, the devil isn't buying stock on the NYSE last I heard, so what are you talking about?"

"Jake Hawkins!" she spat. "Who else do you know with the resources to do what's been going on around here?"

"*Hawkins?*" he asked in disbelief. "You've been sleeping with Jake Hawkins?"

Kelley nodded. "Often and continuously. The man bought the townhouse right next door to mine in Atlanta and set up housekeeping."

"Jake Hawkins?" Roderick asked, still in disbelief. "In a townhouse? In Atlanta?"

"Well, it is Buckhead, JRock," she hissed. "We're not talking about Bass Place in our old neighborhood."

"Yes—but you—and Hawkins?" The combination still drew confusion.

"Stop saying it like that, JRock," she fussed.

Roderick ran his hand over his head and then covered his face momentarily. "Look, Kelley, I'm the last one to criticize about sleeping with a Hawkins—damn! I wanted to sleep with Jai the moment I first saw her—of course, I didn't know she was Jake Hawkins' daughter then, but you knew who Jake Hawkins was before you got involved with him."

"If you had known who JaiHonnah is, who her family is, would it have made a difference?"

"No, but then Jai isn't her father. I don't know what you see in the man, but you could do better, Kelley. You're a very beautiful and desirable woman."

"Yeah, what do you know? You're only my *little* brother."

"Yeah, right," Roderick snorted.

"Look, aren't you concerned about my relationship with Jake?"

"Yeah, I think you ought to have your hormones adjusted and your head examined. You probably need to have your eyes checked, too."

"I mean from a business standpoint, JRock," she deadpanned. "Not from a personal perspective."

Roderick put his hands on her arms. "Kelley, I trust you. You're extremely good at what you do. You wouldn't do anything to hurt me or the company." He looked at his watch again and rose from the tabletop. He kissed Kelley's cheek, enveloped her in his arms, rocking her gently. "Why don't you come home with me tonight and spend the weekend. You can see Jai and the children."

"No, thanks anyway, JRock."

"Look, it's too late for you to drive to your place. Stay here at the condo tonight and get some sleep. I'll talk with you tomorrow."

"All right, JRock. You have a safe trip home and hug Jai for me. Tell her I miss seeing her around the office."

Roderick released Kelley. "Will do, but I need her hugs more than you do. Come for dinner on Sunday, if you have time. I'm sure Jai would appreciate the company."

"I'll call you, little brother."

"Fine. Have a good night and, sis, about your sin..."

"Yes, what?"

"Go to a nunnery."

Kelley pursed her lips and rolled her eyes, as her brother left.

JaiHonnah lost track of the number of times Roderick missed dinner and came home late. The activities in his office were never discussed when he did manage to make it home before midnight. JaiHonnah was beginning to resent the amount of time he spent away from her and the children. This night was no different, she thought, as she lay in bed waiting to hear his car in the driveway and the garage door opening and closing. She was wide-awake and furious.

Roderick came into the house through the garage door. Mr. Betterman was waiting for him as usual, but the house was otherwise quiet.

"How long ago did Mrs. Baylor retire, Betterman?" he asked, as the older man took his coat, hat and gloves.

"Long enough so that maybe you ought to throw your hat in before you go in," the man said, smiling. "See how many bullet holes you get."

"I'm in the dog house again, huh?"

Betterman nodded in the affirmative. "Mrs. Betterman left dinner in the warmer for you."

"Thanks, Betterman," he said, as he walked into the kitchen.

Roderick only turned on the recess lights and saw the letters from his daughters taped to the refrigerator. He slowly shook his head. How long had it been since he actually spent quality time with them? He was up and out of the house by five in the morning and often didn't return until late at night.

Shelley and Shelby started leaving little love letters for him and he'd take the time to write a response to them. He would creep into their room both morning and night just to plant a kiss on their cheeks. He did the same thing with his twin sons who were now a year old.

He wearily shook his head. He didn't want to eat. He wanted to be near his wife. Leaving the kitchen, he climbed the stairs to the master bedroom.

Roderick slid into bed and slipped his arm around JaiHonnah's waist. She stiffened against his embrace and removed his hand from her breast.

"Honey, I'm sorry," he whispered, planting a kiss on her back and neck. JaiHonnah moved away from him. "Jai, baby, please. I said I'm sorry."

"Don't 'baby' me, Roderick!" she hissed. "I don't see why you even bothered to come home tonight! It's nearly one in the morning!"

"JaiHonnah," he tried again. "What do you want me to say? I had a meeting that went later than I thought it would. I had every intention of coming home early. It's been a hellified day. I came home because this is where I want to be. I want to be with you."

"Be with me?" she huffed. "Roderick, you haven't *been* with me in weeks!"

"I'll make it up to you, honey. I'll break out some time and we can get away for a day, maybe two. We could bring the *Indian Princess* and dock her here—"

"Pencil me in, so to speak? Well thanks, but no thanks! Pencils have erasers! I wouldn't want you to accidentally rub me the wrong way! Go to sleep, Roderick! Saturday is another work day at JR Baylor Limited, remember!"

Roderick exhaled deeply and turned onto his back. There was a cold edge to her voice signaling his efforts to make love with her would be an exercise in futility. She had edged away from him and turned her back. They never had so much as a disagreement since they married. Her distancing herself from him now deeply worried him.

Was it all worth it? Was building the business worth losing his wife and family? He lay motionless, shuddering at the thought. Maybe if he discussed what was going on, she might understand, but he didn't want her to worry. After all, she had the children to consider and another baby on the way. How could he tell her that her father might be trying to raid his company or undermine his business? He couldn't even tell Kelley how worried he was about her relationship with Jake Hawkins. The next few weeks would be crucial and he had to stay focused.

He had a lot of unspent energy built up and JaiHonnah's mesmerizing scent was driving him to distraction. Still, she was shutting herself off from him. That was never going to be allowed to continue.

Kelley pulled herself out of a light sleep and flipped on the security monitor. She hit the button, opening the door. As the elevator ascended, she rose from the bed and put on a robe. As she waited for the elevator doors to open, she rubbed her face to clear her bleary eyes.

"Tarnation, woman! Every damn time I look around, you're not where you're supposed to be! Now this boardroom business has got to stop! Bedroom business is more important! Man can't get a decent night's sleep without having to fly clear cross the damn country! Now I'm tired! Let's go to bed!"

Kelley would have laughed if she didn't know Jake Hawkins was serious. She was scheduled to be back in Atlanta that night, but when the meeting lasted so late, she decided to stay in Washington. Jake flew to Washington just to sleep with her. These days they slept together more nights than not since that first night in October. Since then, she dated other men, but Jake would somehow always show up and scare the other men away. Kelley was beginning to wonder whether she had some sign painted on her forehead that read: PROPERTY OF BLACKHAWK. He was everywhere she was, almost before she got to wherever she was going. This was getting to be a serious problem. Still, how the hell did he know where she was anyway?

"Well, are you coming to bed or what?" Jake roared.

Kelley turned her head slightly to look at Jake standing in the doorway of the bedroom, wearing only his Stetson and his cowboy boots with silver spurs. He was a strikingly handsome man, even when he was nude. She shook her head slowly and rose wearily from her perch on the edge of the sofa arm. She sauntered toward him.

"Lose the spurs, cowboy. They cut up the sheets," she said, ducking under his arm as she breezed by him.

"Tarnation, woman, I gotta have something to get a grip with! I'll buy you new sheets!" he roared, as he slammed the bedroom door shut and followed her to the bed. Watching the sway of her impressive hips, he suddenly caught his second wind.

JaiHonnah rolled over and couldn't believe her eyes. She blinked several times to assure herself she wasn't dreaming. Roderick was still in bed. He was turned on his side, supporting his head on the palm of one hand and looking at her.

"Good morning," he said, grinning.

"Good morning," she said, suspicion coating her voice and not sure she was fully awake.

Roderick caressed her face and kissed her gently on the lips. "I'd almost forgotten how good it makes me feel to watch you sleeping beside me and watch the sun rise when you smile at me. You're beautiful, Mrs. Baylor." He reached his free hand under the cover and rubbed her protruding belly. "How is our littlest Baylor this morning?"

"Active," she said drolly. "Roderick, it's nearly eight in the morning. What are you doing here?"

Roderick laughed. "I live here or did you forget? Remember me? I'm your husband. The one who loves you more than my next breath. Aren't you glad to see me?"

"Don't joke with me, Roderick. I'm in no mood for foolishness."

He continued to rub her stomach and pull himself closer to her, threading a leg between her thighs. "Neither am I. I want my wife back. I need her and I miss her. More importantly, I love her. You want to punish me for my absence and my neglect—fine. Whip me, beat me, and I'll take it like a man, but tell me I can't touch you, can't love you, and you've got a fight on your hands, Mrs. Baylor. I'm in love with you and crave you too much to even consider the thought of losing you."

The tears threatened to spill over in JaiHonnah's eyes. Roderick had not said he loved her in so long she almost forgot what his voice sounded like when he spoke those words. The words still had the same effect. He thrilled and excited her beyond belief. She loved him deeply and didn't want to lose him to become a corporate widow; a woman whose husband lived only for the next big deal. She wondered where those days had gone when they worked together, side-by-side, sharing their triumphs together. Finally, the tears did fall and Roderick kissed them away.

"God, I love you, Jai," he whispered vehemently against her ear, as she wept.

"I was beginning to wonder whether you still did or not. You're never home. I thought you were trying to avoid me because I've gotten so big. That maybe you didn't find me desirable anymore," she sobbed.

Roderick raised JaiHonnah's nightgown and began kissing her bulging stomach in several places. "If anything, Mrs. Baylor," he said between soft kisses, "you're more beautiful than before, but now there's just a little bit more of you to love." Her soft scent began to intoxicate him and he let himself move to the rhythm of his need. Instantly, like a drummer's stick, his manhood pulsated and beat against his abdomen.

JaiHonnah stroked Roderick's head as he kissed her abdomen, exciting her and bringing her love-starved body back to life. She closed her eyes, letting the sensations rise from her core.

"How long have you been awake?" she asked.

Roderick squeezed her hand around his engorged phallus. "That long," he whispered in her ear and then trailed his hot, wet kisses down her neck to her shoulder. "I haven't been able to sleep all night. I want you so badly I wanted to love you while you were sleeping."

JaiHonnah stroked him generously and heard his deep-throated groan against her neck. Roderick's abdomen concaved in tight jerks, straining against the painful pleasure of his wife's skillful touch. He wanted to get inside her, to meld with her, but he wanted to savor every minute of their intimacy. The hardness of her nipples in his mouth nearly sent him into oblivion, but he knew that the best was yet to come. He wasted no more time getting there. He buried himself inside her, seeking the sweet nectar only she could deliver. He did not have long to wait. JaiHonnah's thighs tightened against him and her belly rose and fell fitfully as he kissed and nibbled her. Her moans of pleasure rose to a peak, as she breathlessly panted his name. The passion in her voice thrilled him and intensified his need for her. Nothing was more important to him at that moment than his wife and family.

When the third orgasm gripped her, she could take no more. Roderick rolled her onto him and she immediately sheathed him without preliminaries, causing them both to shudder in open-mouthed ecstasy. Roderick braced her back against his raised thighs as she rode him as regally as if she were astride her stallion Hawk. He felt the power within his loins growing beyond his control. His attempts to hold on to his sanity were waning, as his hips moved like a bucking bronco in slow motion. Finally, exquisitely, she tamed him and he roared his pleasure, as did she.

"Have mercy! Have mercy!" Jake roared against his thunderous release. His spurs dug into the bed, ripping the sheets again. "Give me strength! Woman, what you do to me!"

Kelley breathlessly panted, trying to control what little air was left in her lungs before she passed out. The man beneath her had the power. He was the only man who could—with a touch, a kiss, a caress—make her forget her name. His very presence shattered her resolve. He'd simply walk into a room and consume her with his eyes alone. He knew all the right buttons to push. Jake Hawkins was her Achilles heel. She couldn't think with him buried so deep inside her.

Kelley dismounted Jake and strode toward the bathroom.

"Where you goin', woman?" he roared.

"To hell in a hand basket!" she flung over her shoulder, as she went into the bathroom and slammed the door.

"Tarnation!" Jake bellowed, as he fell back heavily against the bed.

The woman had him by the balls—literally and figuratively, he knew. He couldn't sleep without her beside him, not that he did any sleeping when she was. Something was wrong though. He could feel it. Her body, and how she wielded it to captivate him, was still a mystery to him, but he knew when something was on her mind. He would have to find out what it was and eliminate it before whatever it was became a problem. He was well practiced at removing a problem before it became a threat, but with Kelley, practice didn't make perfect. She could turn him on with a wink of her beautiful eyes. Her velvet-smooth skin and voluptuous body had risen more than his blood pressure like no woman since Skai.

Kelley and Skai were, of course, nothing alike, except they both held his heartstrings firmly in their fingers. Skai was his dream. Although he was only seventeen when he met her, and she was twenty-one, she bore four children: two boys, Jacob and Adam, and two girls, LaiLoni Skai and JaiHonnah. He lost Skai to cancer because he wasn't paying attention. He was too busy trying to build a life for them, an empire.

Jacob Junior, his first born, grew up angry at him because of his inability to spend time with him. His second child, his daughter, LaiLoni Skai, was kidnapped from the clinic the day after her birth and never found. His third child, Adam, grew quiet and introspective. Although he loved all of his children equally, his beautiful JaiHonnah was all heart, warm and caring, but he pushed her too hard.

He lost so many years of his children's youth and his second child, LaiLoni. Absolute power, blind ambition, and consummate control were the driving forces fueling him back then in the early days. Now he had it all, but not anyone to share it with. His triumphs were hollow victories that now held little, if any, of his interests.

What did consume his interest now was Kelley Baylor. Nothing about her didn't hold his attention. She was a bold, strong, classy, and brassy woman. Astute in business, clear about her goals and direction, and a tenacious competitor. Damned if he didn't admire her and—damn it! He loved her. He didn't just want her to warm his bed or need her to stroke his ego; she was in his blood.

Kelley came out of the shower wrapped in a towel. She entered the bedroom and saw Jake's massive, masculine, nude body still stretched out on the rumpled bed. He had his hands laced behind his head and one knee raised. She caught her breath. Just the sight of him caused her nature to rise. He was still wearing his Stetson just covering his eyes and chewing on an unlit cigarillo clenched between his pearl-white teeth. He seemed to be deep in thought and did not look at her when she sat before the vanity to brush her hair. She had to think how to do what had to be done. It was killing her inside, but it had to happen. There was no other choice.

"Come to bed, dahlin," Jake growled in a raspy voice.

The lowered timber of his voice sent needful chills flooding through her. "No, Jake, I think that we have run our course."

Jake's brows knitted, as he raised his head a few inches off the pillows to look at Kelley from under his Stetson. She was sitting at the vanity brushing her long, thick hair. He could see her face reflected in the mirror before her.

"The hell you say," he growled, resting his head back against the pillows.

Kelley looked in the mirror and could see Jake biting on the twitching cigarillo.

"I mean it, Jake. I don't think we should see each other anymore."

"You think too much, woman. Now come to bed!"

"You're not listening to me, Jake. Coming to bed with you would be easy, but it's not going to change anything. I've let myself become too deeply involved with you and it's hurting my business and my family. Something has to give."

"You're not sleeping with your family and I don't give a damn about your business!"

"Well, I care about them both, Jake Hawkins!" Kelley bristled. "They make me who I am!"

Jake raised his head slowly and looked at the scowl on Kelley's face. His eyes closed to a menacing slit, his jaw tightened around the cigarillo, and his nostrils flared. His breathing was slow and deliberate. "Get in bed, Kelley Baylor! If you need an answer to who you are, I'll show you! You're *my* woman! Nothing between here and heaven or hell is going to change that fact! Now if you think I'm going to let Baylor Industries stand between us, think again. I'll crush that damn company into the dust before I'll let that happen. I won't let you walk away from me."

Kelley whipped around on the stool. Her brows knitted and her eyes bored into Jake. "Maybe that's what you're trying to do! Maybe that's why you've been sleeping with me so you could raid Baylor Industries!"

"I don't do business in the bedroom! And, if I wanted Baylor Industries or any of your brother's other companies, I could have taken them from him a year ago, two years ago, five years ago!"

"Why didn't you? What stopped you?"

Jake relaxed slightly. "I have my reasons," he said more quietly. "Now are you coming to bed?"

"No, Jake, I'm not!"

Chapter Six

"WHO WAS ON THE TELEPHONE, honey," JaiHonnah asked, as Roderick hung up the telephone in the kitchen.

Distracted, he didn't focus on her question.

"Roderick, what is it?" she asked, as she cut up a head of cabbage.

"Uh, nothing, honey. It was Kelley. She's not coming to dinner. She's in Atlanta," he said distractedly.

"Atlanta? I thought you said she was going to be in town until your meeting next week."

"Yes, uh, that's what I thought, but she suddenly decided to go back. Said something about the devil getting into her . . ." his voice trailed off, as he recalled his conversation with his sister on Friday night.

JaiHonnah noticed Roderick's thoughtful expression and turned, squarely facing her husband. She lodged one hand on her hip and knitted her brow. "It must run in the family," she sniffed saucily.

Roderick's eyes shifted to his wife and a grin curled his lips and mustache. He moved slowly to within a breath of JaiHonnah, spanned her hips with his hands, and looked down into her sparkling eyes. "Yes, ma'am, it does," he said slowly an octave lower than his usual tone. "And this devil is going to get into you again tonight." He bent to plant a kiss on her lips before someone loudly cleared his throat.

"Uh, that's what got you two into trouble in the first place," Ice said, laughing.

"Uh-huh," Roderick snorted, as he kissed JaiHonnah again. "I can't stay away from trouble."

"Trouble? Who's in trouble?" Chuck Montgomery asked, coming into the kitchen with his wife, Vivian, and chomping on an apple.

"Them," Ice nodded toward JaiHonnah and Roderick. "Every time I come in here they're at it again. Man can't keep his hands off her."

"Humph, I know the feeling." Chuck grinned, kissing Vivian on the back of the neck and rubbing her protruding stomach.

Ice shook his head slowly. "Looks like a baby factory around here. Man, y'all already got a basketball squad."

"Yeah, we're working on having an opposing team," Chuck said, laughing.

"When do we eat?" Ice asked. "Roz and my kids are still down in the barn with your livestock."

"Shortly," Roderick laughed. "I just need to make the coleslaw, if Chuck would stop eating up the ingredients."

"Man, since Vivian's been pregnant, I've been eating everything I get my hands on. She's barely gained a pound, but I've put on ten," Chuck said.

"It's those judicial robes. They hide a multitude of sin," Vivian deadpanned.

"What's it like being a judge?" Ice asked.

"Sometimes very gratifying and sometimes very frustrating. Now I know what Judge Ito felt. Sometimes I want to send opposing counsel back to kindergarten and tell them to try it all over again."

"What about this new partner your law firm is bringing in? I understand from Bill—"

Vivian held up one hand. "Hold on, JRock. Remember. My name may still be on the masthead, but it's not my firm anymore and I can't tell you anything about one lawyer verses another."

"Oh, yeah, I forgot, the appearance of impropriety," he said.

"You've got it. Maybe you should consider studying the law, JRock. You're getting good at this."

Roderick laughed. "Uh, Viv, I had a good teacher. Maybe now that you're also teaching at G-Town, I can come take your class."

"Oh, no, he's busy enough as it is," JaiHonnah interjected quickly. "I want him to lighten his load, not increase it."

"Perhaps we should stick to safer territory," Roderick said, laughing. "Have you considered Weight Watchers, Chuck?"

Everyone laughed and then settled down in Roderick and JaiHonnah's new, ultramodern kitchen.

"The place is beautiful, Jai," Vivian said, looking out over the Wicomico River.

"I love it," Chuck agreed. "The Admiral told me he stayed here for a few days."

"David Robinson was in town?" Vivian asked. "You never mentioned it, Chuck."

"Sorry, honey, but you've been so busy; I didn't want to ask you to have a dinner party for him."

"He didn't have much time anyway," Roderick added. "He was speaking at the Naval Academy and only had an overnight visit. I barely had time to spend entertaining him. Jai and the children ended up having to do most of the work. He said he'd make a special trip back just to see you preside over your courtroom though, Viv."

"Well, he'll get a piece of my mind before that," Vivian said, laughing. "I'll call Akeem and ask him to deliver that message personally on the court," she joked.

"You would do that, too, wouldn't you, Judge?" Ice asked.

"With a quickness, Wesley," Vivian answered.

Roderick listened to the banter, but he knew this was probably the last free time he would have in a very long time. Vivian taught him to play chess and now he had some very important moves to make.

"Good afternoon, Mr. Baylor," Kiran Suarez said, as Roderick entered the familiar conference room at Vivian's old law firm for a luncheon meeting with his new attorney. "I'll be with you in a moment," she said, as she continued a conversation on her cell phone.

Kiran Suarez, Roderick observed, was an attractive woman, though she had an edge about her. She had piercing eyes like someone that could look right through him, and did not suffer fools readily.

"I'm sorry about that, Mr. Baylor." Kiran closed her cell phone and then her laptop. "Modern technology isn't always a benefit, but now I have turned off all forms of electronic communications. I have instructed the waiter not to disturb us until I call for him. I've taken the liberty of ordering this white wine before you arrived. I want no distractions during this luncheon."

Kiran poured two glasses of wine and handed one to Roderick.

"I understand how necessary it is to be able to reach out and touch someone at a critical moment. It's not necessary to apologize for having important work to do, Ms. Suarez."

Roderick took a sip of the wine.

"The only person I want to reach out and touch at this moment, Mr. Baylor, is you."

Roderick nearly choked on the wine. He wondered what she had in mind.

"Uh, Ms. Suarez, let me make myself perfectly clear. I'm married to the only woman I'll ever want or love. She satisfies my every need, want or desire. I don't fool around."

"Good. I've seen your wife before. She was the first runner up at the Miss America Pageant years ago. She's gorgeous. I'd probably be more interested in sleeping with her than you, Mr. Baylor, so while we're on the subject of 'making things perfectly clear,' let me state this for the record: I'm an only child. My father wanted a boy, and he got it. I'm not sweet, cuddly or cute. I don't stroke a man's ego or hold a woman's hand without a clear purpose in mind. I'm here to do a job *for* you, not *on* you. I don't wear my homosexuality as a badge of courage or my heterosexuality as a badge of honor. I am a sexual being, however. I feel gratification from both sexes equally. I don't have a preference.

"I've spent seven years litigating cases before the Securities and Exchange Commission, the Internal Revenue Service, every federal circuit court in this country, and the United States Supreme Court. I've also practiced international law and I haven't lost a case stateside or in the international arena, nor do I intend to. I've handled both civil and criminal cases. I've turned down two offers of appointments to circuit courts and countless offers to join prestigious law firms until I received an offer I've coveted from Bill Chandler to join Alexander, Carter, Chandler, Charles and Lightfoot, PA. I'm independently wealthy and I don't really need to work for a living, but I'm a damn good lawyer. Now, that's what you'll be getting for my admittedly high fee. If you have a moral or ethical problem with anything I've said or want other legal counsel, I'm sure this firm will accommodate you."

Roderick breathed a sigh of relief. "Ms. Suarez, I believe my money will be well spent."

"Good. Now let's get down to business. You're a crapshooter, Mr. Baylor. I know because it takes one to know one. You're about to crap out and you haven't taken the necessary steps to stay in the game. You're a Darden School of Business, summa cum laude, grad. You've built an impressive business on the roll of the dice and you've been winning. Now why are you holding back?"

"No matter how good it sounds, I do have a conscience and, as I mentioned before, a wife I love very much. Her father and I have been going head-to-head in the business arena for years. When I started this business, I didn't know Jake Hawkins, except by reputation. Like everyone else in the master's program, we studied the moves of people like him. To me, he was an enigma. He started with nearly nothing and grew an empire on sheer will, tenacity, and cunning. In fact, he was my mentor without knowing it. I wrote my thesis in college about his company, followed the type of bold moves he made, and started emulating many of them.

"When I met my wife, JaiHonnah, I didn't know she was his daughter. When I found out, it was too late. I was already in love with her. Jai fiercely loves her father and I love her. In order to do what has to be done to save my business, I would have to go after many of the same projects one of her father's companies, BlackHawk Builders, is after. It would be open warfare with Jai right in the middle.

"I bought my way onto BlackHawk's board of directors so I could avoid this type of problem, reduce the impact, and keep me and Hawkins from going at each other's throats. Now I think the man has no bounds to his hypocrisy. He's tossed another die into the game, namely, my sister, Kelley. Unfortunately, I believe she's falling in love with the man. She's loyal to me, but, if I go after him, she may find it necessary to choose between her love for him and her love for me and our family. That would tear her apart. Therein lies my dilemma."

A faintly cold smile came to her thin lips. "Surely, Mr. Baylor, you're not going to let a little thing like family loyalty to your wife and your sister stand in the way of your being all you can be, now are you?"

The question startled Roderick, but he understood it. "It's not a little thing to me, but—"

"Still, you're going to kick ass and take names," she said with a gleam in her eyes.

Roderick's stoic expression didn't change. "Yes, ma'am, I'm going to do just that. If Jake Hawkins wants to lose his daughter's love and Kelley's, then he'll roll that dice, not me."

"If it's not Jake Hawkins, who's after you?"

Roderick looked at her quizzically and she noticed.

"Mr. Baylor, you didn't get to where you are without having to kick a lot of ass. Jake Hawkins may not be the one behind this effort to destroy you. If not him then who is?"

"I've made a practice of knowing my enemy and my business. I don't believe I've crossed anyone who would hold a grudge."

"When you came in, I was on the phone with my contacts at the Securities and Exchange Commission (SEC). It seems that the entity buying up your stock and selling it short is offshore."

"Foreign?" he asked in disbelief.

"Precisely. I haven't got a line on the principles or the investors. They've covered themselves very carefully in shell and holding companies. It's a common cloaking device and a real no brainer. I'd strongly suggest you rethink your past business and personal dealings and see whether you can come up with a reason for this assault. Connect the dots, Mr. Baylor."

When Roderick returned to his office, he was still deep in thought. Nothing he had done in his business or career would have brought about this type of attack—or could it? he wondered. He picked up the telephone and hit a speed-dial number.

"Kelley," he said when she answered. "Have you seen Lionel Porter around Atlanta lately?"

"Porter? No, not lately. He and his family have been abroad, I understand. Vacationing in Europe is what I heard at a cocktail party a few days ago. Why do you ask?"

"Something Kiran Suarez said. She asked me to think about people I've crossed both personally and professionally."

"He fits the bill on both counts. He slept with your former wife and you completed a hostile takeover of his business, but who is Kiran Suarez?"

"Our new legal representation."

"Oh, what's she like?"

"The woman defies description."

"That's profound."

"Exactly, so is she—penetrating and serious," Roderick said, laughing.

"Sounds like you like her."

"I do, yes, but it wouldn't matter one bit whether I did or not. She's someone who I think we can respect."

"Well, baby brother, you're a good judge of character. If you respect her that's good enough for me."

"I'm also a good listener, Kelley. You want to talk about why you suddenly flew back to Atlanta?"

"I told you. The devil made me do it. Look, I've got to go. I've got meetings back-to-back."

"Kelley, one more thing."

"What is it?"

"I've altered my master plan. If Hawkins is in the mix, I'm going to have to take him down. I wanted you to know that up front."

"You didn't have to tell me, JRock. You do you. Do whatever you have to do. I'll stand by you."

"I love you, sis, and I'm sorry."

"I love you, too, little brother."

They hung up and Kelley sat back in her chair. She swiveled in her seat to look out her floor-to-ceiling office window at Peachtree Center overlooking the City of Atlanta. Life in Atlanta was enjoyable, especially because Jake was around. He was her center, the one with whom she looked forward to spending her evenings and her nights. Now that would be no more. She didn't know when the first tear fell, but she found herself grabbing for a handful of tissue. Squeezing her eyes shut to brace against the pain, slowly, by degrees, she got control of her emotions. A quick check of her face in a compact mirror revealed she had to freshen her makeup. She took a deep breath and pushed an intercom button.

"Yes, Ms. Baylor," a voice came through the speaker.

"Chad, see if you can get a line on Lionel Porter for me."

"Covert or overt?"

"Covert. I want to know everything he's been doing since he left the company."

"Timetable?"

"Three days."

"Will do."

They hung up and then her executive assistant phoned.

"Yes, Bessy, what is it?"

"A special delivery, ma'am. May I bring it in?"

"Yes."

Bessy entered wearing a broad smile and carrying a huge bouquet of flowers. She handed a leather, letter-sized pouch to Kelley and rested the flowers on Kelley's credenza. Kelley opened the pouch and read the contents. Suddenly, she broke into laughter, startling Bessy.

"Ms. Baylor, are you all right?" Bessie asked, seeing the tears and hearing the laughter.

"Yes, Bessie, I'm fine. Seems I now own a textile mill that manufactures sheets, towels, and other linens." She laughed through her tears.

Bessie smiled knowingly. "Must be that handsome Mr. Hawkins," she swooned. "Sure wish I had someone like him pressing my sheets." She winked at Kelley and started toward the door. "Oh, by the way, he's called every hour. Are you sure you don't want to talk with him?"

Kelley nodded in the affirmative. "Yes, I'm sure."

"Okay." Bessy shrugged. "Still, you know that's not going to stop a man like him."

"I know, but maybe he'll get the message soon." She sighed. "He's a man who enjoys the company of women. He'll move on to another conquest."

"Ha! Fat chance," Bessie scoffed, as she slipped through the door.

Kelley looked at the papers in her hand then tossed them on her desk. She abruptly stood and dug her hands in her pockets as she looked out of her top-floor windows. The thought of Jake with another woman deeply bothered her, more deeply than she cared to admit. He didn't or wouldn't get it, though. It wasn't about the sheets or his silly spurs or Stetson hat. It was a question of loyalty. Loyalty to her brother and her family. For the first time in her life, she knew what loving and losing meant, and it hurt like hell. Maybe it was a good thing she had only felt this way once in her lifetime, because experiencing this type of pain once was more than enough to last a lifetime.

"Jai, why don't you put that beautiful body of yours in some undeserving glad rags and come into town? You can take me to dinner and dancing."

"You buying, handsome?"

"I could be persuaded. It's going to cost you though."

"Oh, how much?"

"Uh-uh, not money. I want your body. I thought we'd spend the night at the condo—all night. I like the way I make your belly rise."

She giggled. "Roderick, you're wicked."

"Baby, you ain't seen nothin' yet. So is it a date?"

"You got any fresh fruit and whipped cream?"

"Chilling as we speak."

"Hold the thought, lover. I'll see you shortly."

They hung up and Roderick leaned back in his chair. His wife was everything he wanted and his family was his pride and joy. He was a happy man. The deceit and treachery of the past with his ex-wife, Monique, was a faded memory. Now he knew what real joy was. What real love was.

Suddenly, something dawned on him. *Monique*, he thought. *Could she be involved in trying to destroy my company?* She was certainly vindictive enough and she had soaked him for as much money as she could get, but what would she have to gain from seeing him destroyed? He reached for the telephone.

"Kristy, see if you can get Monique Baylor on the telephone for me, please."

"Yes, sir, but she's not in the country. She called a week ago to tell your daughters she'd bring them something from Europe. She didn't leave a number where she could be reached, but she said she'd be gone for some time."

"Thanks, Kristy. Forget about that call."

"Yes, sir."

They hung up and Roderick sat back in his chair steepling his fingers at his lips. Kiran said the company was offshore, he recalled, but Monique was no financial wizard. If she were involved, she'd have to have help. Lionel Porter had an intimate affair going on with Monique while he was still married to her. He took Porter's company away from him in a hostile takeover. Porter was in Europe, too, supposedly with his family on vacation. Roderick wondered whether there was a connection. *"Connect the dots,"* Kiran said. He picked up the telephone, again.

"Yes, sir."

"Kristy, get the number for Slade Richardson at Richardson Investigations and Security. They're the investigators Vivian's law firm uses."

"Yes, sir, right away."

"One body delivered," JaiHonnah said, seductively standing at Roderick's office door.

To him, she looked fantastic in her bright red, maternity, after-five attire. He let out a slow, loud whistle. "You are one sinfully sexy sister, Mrs. Baylor."

She sauntered toward him. "You're a real heart-stopper yourself, handsome. Now do I deliver first or do you," she cooed, straddling his lap and seductively licking at his lips.

Roderick grinned and ran his hands up her thighs. He looked up into her devilish expression. She wasn't wearing any panties under that sexy frock.

Roderick groaned at the feel of her hot, bare bottom on his lap. His nature rose the moment she walked in the door. He wanted to make love to her right then and there, but he had to hold off. He had to tell her what he was about to do.

"Lady, I need sustenance to handle this. We'd better eat dinner first or I won't make it through the night—and I intend to make it through the night," he said with a husky voice against her lips.

"Then let's get going, big boy. I want you to have a seven-course meal, but I want to be your desert."

"I never tire of your flavor, Mrs. Baylor," he whispered and kissed her deeply.

Roderick and JaiHonnah sat at a candlelit table for two at a restaurant not far from his office. They had a stunning view of the Potomac River and the jets taking off and landing at Reagan National Airport. Roderick was waiting for the right moment to talk with JaiHonnah about his concerns and what he thought he needed to do. She sat gazing at him and he didn't want to change the mood. She was so beautiful, sensuous, and sexy. It was hard to imagine she didn't win the national beauty pageant. Her pregnancy gave her a golden glow. There would be time later, he thought. For now, he just wanted there to be nothing but love between them. When the live band began to play, they danced the night away and went home early to their condo atop their business offices. He had to have her.

Later, as they lay in bed, Roderick cuddled JaiHonnah close to his body. He heard her quiet breathing and knew she was sleeping peacefully. The thought of disturbing her quiet rest was more than he wanted to have happen then after such a fun-filled date night. He rubbed her stomach and felt their baby moving in her belly. The sensation thrilled him and he stroked his active child nestled in the warmth of his wife's womb.

He furrowed his brow. How could he do this to them? How could he deliberately plot and plan to take down Jake—Jai's father and his baby's grandfather? Were he still alive, he would never do something like this to his own father. How could he do it to Jai's father and hope to keep his growing family intact and unscathed? It was an impossible situation.

Roderick felt JaiHonnah wiggle her butt against him. When his phallus stood at attention, he moved closer, putting his hand to her breast. He caressed the full circumference, worrying her nipples. She felt velvet smooth and silky soft.

"What's bothering you, honey?" she asked, raising his hand to her lips and kissing his palm.

"Your butt, baby. You're driving me crazy," he groaned against her ear.

"We haven't made love like this in a very long time, but I sense something is on your mind."

"Yeah, something is," he groaned. "I want you so much, I can't get enough."

"I'm right here next to you. I'm not going anywhere. You're acting as if we don't have a minute to spare. Like we have some reason to hurry. We're all right, aren't we, Roderick? I mean, you're not tired of me or disappointed because we have to find creative ways to make love because I'm pregnant, are you?"

Roderick held her closer. "No, baby, we're fine. I'm just hungry for you."

JaiHonnah turned her head and looked over her shoulder at him. "That's the truth, Roderick?"

He thought before he answered. Maybe he should tell her now what he was up against. Trying to divert her to keep her out of the melee was his goal, however. He didn't want her to have to divide her loyalties. What she would do if she knew, he wondered. His late nights and early mornings at the office were already putting a strain on their marriage, pulling at the fragile fabric of the life they were trying to build together. Making the concession to accept her father's gift of the estate was his attempt to reduce the acrimony rejecting the gift would surely have caused. He transferred money to her father's account to cover the cost of the property, but her father refused it.

Now fighting her father over possession of his companies could raise more problems between them. Problems he didn't want or need, but he was determined. He would not become one of Jake's puppets, like his sons, Jacob Junior and Adam. He would stand or fall on his own merit. That was the way he grew up and he saw no reason to change.

"Yes, honey, that's the truth. There's nothing bothering me, except my unrelenting desire for you," he whispered. "Now are you going to talk all night or are you going to let me love you?"

Something in Roderick's voice in the night told her not all was well, but her urgent need for her husband, as he kissed her neck, wiped away any additional questions.

Chapter Seven

"DEER HAVEN."

"Mr. Roderick Baylor, please."

"I'm sorry, but Mr. Baylor isn't available. Would you like to speak with Mrs. Baylor?"

"Uh, yes."

"Who shall I say is calling?"

"Melody from Attorney Kiran Suarez's office."

"One moment please."

Shortly JaiHonnah picked up the telephone. "Hi, Melody."

"Hi, Jai, how are you?"

"Just fine, what can I do for you?"

"Ms. Suarez wants to meet urgently with Mr. Baylor."

"Oh, what's going on?"

"You haven't heard?"

"Heard? Heard what, Melody?"

"Jai, uh, I'm sorry, maybe I shouldn't have said anything."

"Well, you have now, so tell me, what's so urgent?"

Melody related everything to JaiHonnah and she listened, astounded by what was going on. She was still furious when Roderick came in late that evening.

"I'm your wife, Roderick Baylor, and your partner! Not a child you have to protect from harm!" she snapped.

"I understand that, honey, but—"

"But nothing! You and Jake think too much alike for my comfort! All this time you've been worrying about how I would handle it and you never gave me the chance to tell you what I think. I do think, you know!"

"All right, Jai, I do know. I wasn't trying to treat you like a child."

"No, you've been treating me like a mushroom; keeping me in the dark and feeding me shit, just like Jake used to do! Only you've added a twist. You're keeping me barefoot and pregnant and living on the outskirts of your life! Well, that's over, Mr. Baylor!"

"Jai, it's not that I don't want you with me, it's just that you've made a beautiful and loving home for all of us. You can work when or if you want to, but the children need you now during their formative years."

"Oh, no you don't, Roderick. Our family has two parents! You want me to be the one shaping their minds. Well you were a great parent before I came along. You can stay home and be the house frau, the stepford wife and I'll work and make a living for both of us!"

JaiHonnah stormed out of the room and Roderick slumped in a chair. He hadn't seen her so angry before.

JaiHonnah paced, trying to cool her temper. If Jake Hawkins were involved in trying to destroy the man she loved, then her father would have to deal with her! "I didn't just sit on the hood of his Stutz Bearcat without learning a thing or two about BlackHawk," she said aloud to the air.

JaiHonnah sat in the kitchen, pondering what Roderick told her. Something didn't make sense, though. True, her father was a corporate raider, but, usually, before he commenced a hostile takeover, he would make the company a generous offer. That's how he handled taking over Chapman Forestry Industries, the company previously owned by her ex-husband, Calvin Chapman and his father, Clarence Chapman. She was intimately involved in those negotiations, so she knew how her father operated. He was cunning, but usually very fare.

Roderick didn't mention anything about Jake making an offer to him first, and that added to her confusion about the entire scenario. Just as confused as she was about Jake's relationship with Kelley. She picked up the telephone to speed-dial her father's cell phone. Still, she got no answer. She had been calling all morning. Then she tried the number in Texas.

"Hawk House," Ezra answered.

"Hi, Ezra, it's Jai."

"How you doin', dahlin?"

"Fine, Ezra. I'm looking for Jake. Is he at home?"

"No, dahlin, your daddy been gone now for quite a spell. Been stayin' in Atlanta mostly. Came home for a hot minute couple days ago fit to be tied. Said somethin' bout a dead man walkin' then he was gone again."

"Who was he angry with, Ezra, do you know?"

"Naw, Ms. JaiHawk, he didn't say."

"Thanks, Ezra. When you speak with him, please tell him that I'm looking for him."

"Sure thing, Ms. JaiHawk, and kiss them children of yours for me."

"I'll do that, Ezra."

JaiHonnah hung up and was still confused. Ezra Neal, twelve years Jake's senior, was her father's friend and confidant. They met in the early days when Jake snatched his younger sister, Mavis, away from an orphanage and ran away, headed for California. They met up with Ezra, an oil-well worker, on the road. Together, they settled in Texas for a while working the oil fields around Galveston. Jake and Ezra were together through Jake's rise in the oil industry and now Ezra took care of Jake's home, estate, and business in Hawkinstown. They were as close as brothers so if Ezra didn't know exactly where Jake was, something was amiss. Trying to find her father was never a problem before. Now it was nearly impossible. She made another call.

"BlackHawk International, how may I direct your call please?"

"This is J. Reise Hawkins Baylor. Connect me with Jacob Hawkins, please."

"One moment, please."

JaiHonnah waited and then the operator came back.

"I'm sorry, Ms. Hawkins, but Mr. Jacob Hawkins is out of the country and cannot be reached. I will make sure he gets the message that you're trying to reach him."

"Out of the country? Where is he?"

"I'm not at liberty to divulge that information."

"Then get me Adam Hawkins."

"Yes, ma'am, one minute, please."

Shortly Adam answered.

"Hi, Jai, this is a pleasant surprise."

"Not so pleasant, Adam. I'm trying to reach Dad. Do you know where he is?"

"Sorry, sis. I haven't talked with him, but you sound angry. What's he done now?"

"I don't know. That's what I'm trying to find out."

Adam laughed. "Well, I see that the war is still on between you and Jake."

"And how! Adam, do you happen to know whether Dad has made a move on Baylor Industries? Has he started a takeover attempt?"

"You know Dad as well as I do. He usually doesn't telegraph his moves. Certainly not to me anyway. I only know what he's done *after* he's done it and usually only if I read it in the *Wall Street Journal*. Ask Jacob, maybe he knows something. He keeps up with Dad's moves more than I do."

"I tried to reach him, but he's out of the country somewhere."

"That's funny. He didn't say anything to me about it, but just like Dad, Jacob moves in mysterious ways. If I speak with either of them, I'll tell them you're looking for them. You're all right thought, are you? Nothing's wrong with your family or your pregnancy, right?"

"Thanks, Adam. I'm fine and so is my family. Come see us the next time you're in Washington."

"You mean you're not coming to the board meeting?"

"No, you know I never attend those things."

"I thought since your husband is now on the board of directors you'd naturally want to be there, too."

"No, thank you. I left my voting shares in the RAMOS blind trust. Grandmother has always had my proxy to exercise my vote on the board. I see no reason to change now."

"Okay, JaiHawk. Next time I'm in the country, I'll make a trip just to see you."

"Roderick and your nephews, too."

"Of course. For you, JaiHawk, I'll even be civil to the man," he said and laughed.

"You'd better."

"I love you, too, Jai."

"Back at you, Adam."

They hung up and the telephone rang.

"Deer Haven," JaiHonnah answered automatically.

"Mrs. J. Reise Chapman, please."

"This is J. Reise."

"Oh, Mrs. Chapman, this is Dr. Sheffield at the Willow Clinic."

"Yes, Dr. Sheffield, what may I do for you?"

"Well, I just wanted to report Mr. Chapman has signed himself out of the clinic."

"He's completed his therapy then?"

"Well, no. Not exactly."

"What did he do, exactly?"

"He was making real progress, we thought, but then this man came to see him and shortly after that, he signed himself out against medical advice."

"AMA, huh? You said someone came to see him? Who was the man?"

"He didn't give his name and, of course, visitors don't have to sign in at the clinic. I just thought you should know."

"Thank you, Dr. Sheffield."

"You're welcome, Mrs. Chapman. I hope you and your husband can work things out. You're all he talked about while he was here. He was looking forward to getting back together with you."

A chill went up JaiHonnah's spine when she hung up the telephone. Calvin Chapman had to have known there was no possibility of their getting back together. Certainly, someone should have told him she was now married to Roderick Baylor.

Suddenly she remembered the angry eyes looking at her the day he came to the ranch. He was certainly in a cold rage when she told him he would never own controlling interest in BlackHawk Holding and in order to avoid prosecution for multiple acts of violence against women, he'd have to pay a monetary restitution to each woman and agree to go into therapy. If it hadn't been for Ezra...she shuttered at the thought. Well, she hoped, as long as he made progress, perhaps he could straighten out his life.

Then something else dawned on her. Could her former husband and his father be behind the moves on Baylor Industries? Calvin certainly had the business acumen and probably the resources, too. After all, Calvin was an international financier. She thought about whether she should mention it to Roderick and then changed her mind. She was still furious with him and he had enough to handle. She would look into this personally.

Chapter Eight

SIX PEOPLE SAT AROUND A TABLE in an undisclosed location. The conversation was hushed. The paneled room absorbed all sound.

"Have you put the wheels in motion?" one person asked.

"Yes, I've done as instructed."

"Look, I've put my reputation and considerable financial backing into this enterprise with little or no tangible results."

"There's no reason to concern yourself with that. You'll benefit handsomely for your time and investment. We all will when I head both BlackHawk Holding and Baylor Industries, and Baylor will be out on his ass."

"Good! That's exactly what I wanted to hear."

Everyone nodded simultaneously in agreement.

"Then this is the next step in the plan..."

Jake Hawkins cackled loudly, as he read the *International Business Journal.* The cover story gave him reason for the humor.

Developer Offers Gift of Six Hundred Million to City Officials.

J. Roderick Baylor, former basketball great and entrepreneur, offered the City of Washington, DC, a gift to stem the city's financial woes...sources, close to the recently initiated congressional investigation of developers, said this is an example of the high-powered, high-handed tactics men who think that they are above the law employ for their own financial gain....

"Way to go, boy!" Jake said enthusiastically, and then laughed wickedly. "Now you're in the game."

"Sir, may I do anything else for you?" the very attractive European woman asked, smiling down at Jake as he sat in the wide, deep Jacuzzi.

"Dahlin," he grinned, not looking up at her, "I have everything I need."

The enticing smile on the woman's face slipped as she started to leave. Then she turned back to him.

"Uh, Mr. Hawkins, may I ask a question?"

"Sure, dahlin, what is it?" he asked, without looking at her, as he continued to read the newspaper.

She eased down beside the marble Jacuzzi, dangling her slender fingers in the water.

"Well, we were wondering—me and the other girls—why you haven't taken any of us to bed. When your service called to ask whether accommodations were ready and to confirm the date you were coming to Europe, we thought it would be like the other times. I mean, don't we please you anymore?"

A thumb and forefinger kicked up Jake's Stetson and his brow knitted. "My service alerted you I was coming?"

"Well, yes, sir. Just like they always do."

Jake thought for a moment. His service didn't know where he was. They couldn't have called to alert anyone of his arrival. His mission was supposed to be top secret. Something was afoot and he didn't like the smell of it. He rolled the cigarillo around between his teeth. Then he felt the woman's hand exercising his phallus under the warm, sudsy water. He turned his head and grinned at the woman.

"Dahlin', only one woman knows how to handle that, and she's in Atlanta," he said coldly, still grinning.

The woman removed her hand, stood, and quickly left the room.

Jake tossed the newspaper on the floor and lay back in the warm, bubbling Jacuzzi. Thoughts of Kelley came flooding back to him. It had been weeks since she had walked out on him and she hadn't even returned his calls. This situation with Kelley was getting out of hand. She should be there with him, by his side. To hell with her commitments. Still, she was his woman first, last and always. Still, she wasn't his yet, he reminded himself. She was stubborn as a mule. He'd rectify that little problem very soon. For now, he had other business to attend to—family business of his own.

"This is not a good move, JRock! You've left yourself wide open. Your position is too exposed," Kiran said, stalking his office. She flung the newspaper on his desk. "When I say something is urgent, I expect to hear from you immediately!"

"I knew you were looking for me! I got it from my wife when I walked in the door!"

Kiran stopped pacing and looked toward Roderick. "Look, I didn't know my assistant told JaiHonnah about what was going on. I have to apologize—"

"Damn it! I don't want excuses or apologies!" he raged.

"Look, I understand you're angry. It's a breach of attorney-client confidentiality, but—"

"Angry is an understatement! Do you understand what this is doing to my wife? The very thing I wanted to avoid! If someone wants to try to destroy me piece by piece, day by day, I can take that! What I won't tolerate is bringing my wife into the mix!"

"That's where you're wrong, Baylor! Your wife could help you with this. She's in a perfect position to find out what her father is up to."

Roderick shook his head. "No!"

"Why not?"

"I don't give up that easily, Ms. Suarez. I will not use my wife!"

"You've used her already!" she flung at him.

Roderick's jaw muscle flexed and his eyes blazed. Kiran noticed and relaxed her stance.

"Look, it's been a long day," she relented. "We can take this up tomorrow. In the meantime, it is my considered opinion that you should cease your philanthropic tendencies and altruistic needs as it regards the East of the River Baylor Plaza Park project..."

Roderick rose from his desk. "Your legal opinion is what I want, Ms. Suarez. Baylor Plaza Park will go forward if I have to build it with my bare hands! My business practices are not open for discussion."

Kiran inhaled deeply. "You're right, Mr. Baylor, I have no role in making your decisions. I believe we've covered everything we can this evening. I'll speak with you tomorrow."

She turned on her heels and headed toward the door. Ice held it open for her. She glared at him as she left.

"*Whew!*" Ice released a breath, as he approached Roderick. "Man, I thought you two were going to come to blows." He noticed Roderick's contemplative state. "It's been rough on you, hasn't it, JRock? Rougher than you're letting on."

Roderick lifted his eyes to his oldest friend and leaned his head back against the high-back chair.

"Not as rough as it's been on Jai. Probably with any other man, this situation wouldn't be happening. If she had married a doctor or a painter or a garbage collector, she wouldn't be in the middle of this war between me and her father. Yet, she married someone who is in the same business—competitors, in fact," he said bitterly. "It's tearing her apart."

"I've noticed that, too," came a voice from the doorway.

Ice and Roderick turned to look.

"Savannah," Roderick said, as he stood and rounded his desk.

Dr. Savannah Logan extended her hand. "It's good to see you," she said, smiling. "I was on my way home and saw your car still out front. I figured you were still working late as usual."

Roderick smiled. "Only eight days a week. Uh, have you met my associate, Wesley Greenfield?"

"No, I haven't had the pleasure." Savannah smiled and extended her hand.

"Wesley, this is Dr. Savannah Logan, Jai's doctor. They were in college together."

"A pleasure," Ice said, shaking her hand, "but I think you're my wife's doctor, too. Rosalyn Hunter Greenfield."

"You're right. I am."

"Uh, look, JRock, I've got an early morning meeting at the Baylor Plaza Park site and this doesn't seem to need my presence, so I'll leave now."

"I'll talk with you tomorrow, Ice."

"Later, JRock, and good evening to you, Dr. Logan."

As Ice was leaving the building, a black town car pulled up in front of him, a chauffeur opened the rear door and a man unfolded himself from the car. The light was too dim for Ice to make out the man's face. However, the man studied Ice and finally spoke.

"Is this Baylor's office?"

"Who's asking?"

The man started past Ice who slowed his advance with a hand on the man's chest. The man looked down at Ice's hand and glared at him.

"Oh, it's you," Ice said.

"You look tired, JRock," Savannah said, smiling wanly. "You need to get more rest."

"Thanks, but rest is only an occasional luxury," he said wearily.

"Yes, so I've been reading in the newspapers. You're caught between the proverbial rock and a hard place, no pun intended, JRock."

"Yes, you could say that, but why did you stop by, Savannah?"

"It's about Jai. She's missed a few appointments and I'm concerned."

Roderick came to attention. "I didn't know. She's been under a bit of a strain lately." He looked away.

Savannah caressed his face. "So have you," she said, turning his face back toward hers and looking into his eyes. "You should have Chuck Montgomery give you a good going over."

"Thanks, Savannah," he said, with a loose embrace and a kiss on the cheek. "I'm fine, it's Jai—"

Roderick noticed two figures at the door. He released Savannah and stepped back from her.

"Uh, JRock, sorry to interrupt, but—" Ice started.

"No interruption," Roderick said, looking at the man standing beside Ice. "Jacob, what can I do for you?"

Jacob had observed the intimate moment between the two lovers. He glanced at Roderick, but his attention was riveted on the intoxicating woman with him. Roderick noticed.

"Uh, Dr. Savannah Logan, this is Jacob Hawkins—"

"Jacob needs no introduction, JRock. We've met before. You're Jai's brother, aren't you?" She extended her hand.

He took it and raised it to his lips. "You have me at a disadvantage, Dr. Logan. I'm sure I would have remembered if I'd met such a beautiful woman before," he said, lasciviously eyeing her.

"JaiHonnah and I were at Spelman together," Savannah said. "You used to visit her there."

"That's true, but I don't recall seeing you before. I thought I met most of JaiHonnah's friends."

"Well, we weren't that close then."

"And now?" he asked with a raised eyebrow.

"Now I'm her doctor," Savannah said, feeling uncomfortable under his directed glare. She turned to Roderick. "I'll be going now, Roderick. We'll talk about that other matter tomorrow."

"Fine, Savannah," he said turning to Ice. "Would you see that Dr. Logan gets safely into her car?"

"Sure, JRock," Ice said, taking up a position beside Savannah.

"Nice seeing you again, Jacob," she said, moving toward the door.

"The feeling is mutual, Doctor," he said, his eyes following her quick retreat. It wouldn't be the last time he saw her, he vowed silently. He had only planned a short trip to see his sister, but Savannah Logan was suddenly added to his agenda for a number of reasons. If his brother-in-law was having an affair with her, all the better. He'd take the beautiful doctor away from Roderick, too.

Jacob turned toward Roderick, who stood with a stiff back, head up, and shoulders back. His fists were dug down in his pockets. Jacob sauntered around Roderick while they eyed each other like two fighters in a ring sizing up the other.

"My driver couldn't find your place in Charles County. I wanted to stop by and surprise my sister. She's been trying to reach me."

Roderick looked at his watch. "Jai is probably asleep by now, but I'm on my way home. You can follow me."

Roderick slowed his car as he reached the roadway leading to the estate in Charles County, Maryland. He reached up and pushed a button on the remote control attached to his sun visor and the roadway was suddenly bathed in light. The house was dark except for the lights beaming brightly on the exterior. Roderick pulled into the garage, got out of the car, and waited for Jacob Junior and his chauffeur to join him. When they did, Roderick entered the house and saw Mr. Betterman waiting as usual.

"Good evening, Mr. Baylor," Betterman said without expression.

"Good evening, Betterman. This is Mrs. Baylor's brother, Jacob Hawkins. Would you show his chauffeur to the guest apartment?"

"Yes, sir," he said with a slight bow. "And Mr. Hawkins, sir?"

"I'll show him to one of the guest suites, Betterman. You may turn in for the night."

"Yes, sir," he said again with a slight bow, as he led the chauffeur out to the staff's quarters.

Roderick felt Jacob's piercing eyes on him. He turned slightly and led the way into the library. Roderick laid his briefcase on the desk and went to the liquor cabinet.

"Would you like something?" he asked without turning.

"Tequila, straight," Jacob said, wandering around the expansive library which contained wall-to-wall books and a high ceiling, looking at the titles, figurines, and art on the walls.

It was an impressive library, Jacob thought. Books were carefully shelved ceiling high, wall-to-wall. All manner of topics on business, economics, and the like. The computer disk library was equally as impressive. Clearly, Roderick Baylor carefully studied his chosen field.

Roderick wasn't sure what to make of his brother-in-law's impromptu visit. For the moment, he chose not to query him on his purpose, but to await his approach. He didn't have long to wait.

"Dr. Logan, have you known her very long?" Jacob turned toward Roderick, "and very intimately?"

"The nature of my relationship with Dr. Logan is not open for discussion," Roderick said with an edge to his voice. "What is important is her relationship with JaiHonnah." He handed the glass of tequila to Jacob. "She is exactly what she said. She's Jai's doctor—and friend."

"How convenient to have your wife and your woman on friendly terms."

Roderick's jaw tightened and his eyes narrowed, but he held his temper. He wanted to cold slam the man. "I won't dignify that remark with an answer." He drank his tequila in one shot and slammed the empty glass down on the desk. "If you're ready, I'll show you to your suite."

Jacob gulped his tequila while holding a fixed stare on Roderick. He put down his glass and followed Roderick out of the library, grabbing his luggage as they went.

After Roderick closed the door to Rodney and Reise's bedroom, he walked toward the master bedroom. His temper quelled after seeing his daughters and sons sleeping peacefully. He paused as he opened the door to his bedroom suite. JaiHonnah was asleep. He disrobed and climbed into bed. His wife didn't move, he noticed. She was nowhere near him, but he felt her presence. It was distant and withdrawn from him. She no longer asked him to come home early and did not stir in the mornings when he rose to get ready for work. Whenever he did come home early for dinner, she barely looked at him at the dinner table anymore, leaving the conversation to him and the children. She wouldn't come into the library at night after the children were asleep, while he was working, and she didn't wait up for him to come to bed. He was deeply concerned about how their lives were going, but didn't have the opportunity or make the time to correct the situation.

He fingered JaiHonnah's silky tresses on the pillow and kissed the ends before he closed his eyes.

JaiHonnah lay awake, as usual, until she heard the garage door open and close and heard the exterior door open before she would permit herself to drift into sleep. She sensed when Roderick was near her. His blatant masculinity still enticed her, but the arguments they had of late left her feeling cold and distant. She evaded him to avoid the anger. Too many nights she had to explain to the children why their father was not around. The boys' second birthday had come and gone. Roderick barely made it home from work in time for the party. Vivian and Chuck Montgomery were there along with their children and so were the Baylors, Roderick's siblings and his nieces and nephews. Ice brought his wife, Roz, and their children, too. Roderick was the last to arrive just as they were singing to the boys. She swallowed her anger for the children's sake, but she would not tolerate many more of his absences.

JaiHonnah knew and understood what Roderick was doing. The problem was she didn't agree with his drive and ambition. She saw first-hand what her mother, Skai, suffered when Jake was still building his empire. Too many lonely nights and lost days and then she was gone.

To say her mother died of loneliness was too simplistic. Her mother, a registered nurse, didn't take care of herself as she should have. By the time the cancer was discovered, it was too late.

Jake blamed himself for not being there for Skai to watch over her, but what good could it do after the fact.

Her father and Roderick were a lot alike and that worried JaiHonnah. Would Roderick get so engrossed in his drive to be the best entrepreneur he would neglect her and their family? Could winning be more important than spending time at the children's school plays or taking family vacations? Would they lose the love and the passion they felt for each other so soon?

Less than two years after they were married, they were like two roommates rather than husband and wife. For better or worse, for richer or poorer, in sickness or in health, forsaking all others, *'til death do us part*, she repeated in her head each night. She still loved him fiercely, but something had to change and soon or they would lose each other and everything they were building as a family unit.

Roderick stroked JaiHonnah's hair as she began to awaken. Sometime during the night, she rolled into his arms in her sleep. It was the first time she touched him in far too long. He was awake, thinking she was searching for his love, but he soon discovered she was still asleep. The baby was very active and he felt the kicks through her belly.

When JaiHonnah awoke, she looked at Roderick as if he were a stranger. She didn't speak, as she untangled herself from him and reached for her robe at the end of the bed. She had difficulty standing and Roderick rushed to her aid, but she brushed him off, as she headed for the bathroom. When she returned, she sat at the vanity brushing her hair.

"Jai, I'm taking JR Baylor Holding international," he said, still lying in bed.

JaiHonnah inhaled deeply. "I'm happy for you. I'm leaving tomorrow."

Roderick sat straight up in bed. "Leaving? Where are you going?"

"Home with the children," she said dispassionately, still brushing her hair.

Roderick sprung from the bed and covered the distance between them in a flash. He turned JaiHonnah around to face him.

"You *are* home, Jai! This is our home, not Texas! We're married, remember? We make decisions like this together!"

"Yes, like your decision to take JR Baylor Holding international without consulting me," she said coolly. "That's how *'together'* we are."

The statement dug into him like a knife. She was right. He hadn't consulted her. He searched her eyes for some semblance of warmth and understanding, but none was forthcoming.

"Jai, this is not the time for you to go anywhere. The baby is due any time now. You can't—"

"I can and I will!" she hissed, turning away from him back toward the mirror. "I had Rodney and Reise without you. I can have this baby alone, too."

That statement was the axe that cracked his brain. He took her in his arms and held her close, squeezing her to his body, but she did not yield to him. She remained ridged, as he held her and he felt her distance even more acutely. He kissed her forehead, her eyes, her nose and then her lips, but she would not open to him. His brow was furrowed when he closed his eyes and placed his forehead to hers.

"Honey, I'll do better, I promise. I'll stay home every morning, have breakfast with you and the children, and then take the girls to school. I'll be home every night at six and I'll cut out working on the weekends."

JaiHonnah's heart was breaking, but she eased out of Roderick's arms. She had to stand her ground no matter how much she wanted to melt into his embrace. She rose from the bench unsteadily and started toward the bedroom door.

"Jai, what is it you want me to do?"

"Nothing. Betterman will take us to the airport. If you can find the time, you might want to spend a few minutes with the children—quality time—before we leave. I've given the Bettermans time off while we're away, so you'll have to cook for yourself. Chuck and Vivian have agreed to let me stable the horses on their ranch so the stable hands can take some time off. Since no one will be here, you might want to consider staying in town, but then again, that's completely up to you." She walked out of the bedroom, closing the door behind her.

Roderick closed his eyes and rubbed his hand over his head. His temples were pulsating and his heart was beating wildly. Uncharacteristically, he let everything swirl around him. So much was going on in his life—too much!

JaiHonnah went into the kitchen and put a cup of herbal tea in the Kuerig for herself.

"Not a good morning, huh, honey?" Mrs. Betterman asked, as she prepared breakfast.

JaiHonnah put her arms around the older woman's shoulders and squeezed her. "Not the best I've ever had, Henrietta."

"He loves you, child. He's just tryin' to make his way. Take care of his family the way a man is supposed to do."

"I know that, Henrietta. I know he loves me and I love him more and more each day, but he doesn't have to work as hard and as long as he does." She turned and walked toward the window wall and saw her brother trying to mount Hawk. "Henrietta," she said with some concern, "when did my brother get here?"

Mrs. Betterman joined her at the window. "Oh, him," she said coolly. "Came in with Mr. Baylor last night, Harvey said."

JaiHonnah opened the French door and stepped out onto the deck. Hawk was prancing and bucking so hard JaiHonnah feared

Jacob would be hurt. Hawk would never let Jacob Junior ride him before, but Jacob seemed determined. Finally, Jacob gave up, loudly issuing expletives. JaiHonnah waved and beckoned her brother to come to her.

"Jacob," she said, smiling. "You know Hawk is temperamental."

Jacob frowned at her. "That horse is just plum loco, if you ask me!" He studied her bloated stomach. "Couldn't keep your legs closed, I see," he quipped.

JaiHonnah pursed her lips. "As if you haven't opened a few female's legs in your time. By the way, why aren't you finding someone to make happy?"

"Happy? Is that what you are, Jai, happy?" he snorted.

She knitted her brow and he noticed.

"All right, I'm out of line. So, tell me about Savannah Logan."

JaiHonnah's face filled with confusion. "Savannah? Why would you suddenly ask me about her?"

"I saw her last night in your husband's office sharing an 'unguarded moment.'"

The pain that shot through JaiHonnah paralyzed her. *What was he saying? What 'unguarded moment'?* Her eyes flashed and her thoughts raced. Was Jacob intimating that Savannah and

Roderick were having an affair? Had he caught them together in some compromising position? Was that why Roderick was spending so much time away from her and away from home?

Roderick and Savannah had once been lovers before his marriage to Monique. After his divorce, Savannah and Roderick were close again until she, JaiHonnah, entered the scene and married Roderick.

Her knees felt weak and she found a seat on a nearby glider. She had to stay calm and not let on to Jacob how much his statement crushed her.

"Are you all right, Jai?" he asked with some concern.

"Yes, Jacob. I'm just pregnant, that's all, and as for Savannah, she's my doctor. She and I were at Spelman together. I guess you don't remember seeing here there. She's an obstetrician and gynecologist at Georgetown Medical now. Her brother is Ambassador Jefferson Logan." JaiHonnah felt her hands shaking and put down the mug of tea. She tried to keep her voice even and calm. "So, what brings you to Washington?" she asked, steadying herself.

"Business, of course. Jake wanted me to take care of a few things for him."

"Where is he, Jacob? I've been trying to reach Dad for weeks."

"Working on some deal. He's in Europe. Some top level trade delegation or something. He didn't give me the details. Everyone's scrabbling since the Secretary of State resigned. The President asked Dad to help. Why? What's so important?"

"Uh, nothing. I mean, I wondered whether Dad was trying to raid Baylor Industries. Roderick's been having such a difficult time lately. I thought maybe Dad had something to do with it or knew who did."

"You have to see things clearly, Jai. Your thirty-day boy wonder just passed the thirty-first day. He's not all that he's cracked up to be," Jacob said smugly. "He should have kept on bouncing a ball for a living and not tried to step out of his element into the big leagues where he doesn't belong."

JaiHonnah looked up at her brother with furrowed brow, really seeing him for the very first time. "You're envious of him, aren't you?" A growing realization gripped her.

"Him? Never." He snorted.

I can't lose her, Roderick repeated in his head, as he drove to his office in the thick of the morning rush hour. He called the florist, ordering two dozen, yellow roses be delivered to her by noon. He included a note that said simply, 'I love you. Please don't go'. He couldn't recall the last time he remembered to send flowers to JaiHonnah. He called his office and asked his secretary to rearrange all of his meetings so he would be free by five o'clock. By the time he reached the office, his meetings were scheduled back-to-back, but a phone call changed the carefully laid plans.

"JRock, man, we've got big trouble," Ice said anxiously over the telephone. "I tried to handle this, but—"

"Chill, man. What is it?"

"You'd better come to the site and see for yourself."

"I can't leave now. I've got another meeting within ten minutes—"

"JRock, the inspectors are here and they're threatening to shut down the work. Mallory was hurt on the job and he's on his way to the hospital—"

"I'm on my way," Roderick said, as he hung up the telephone and hurried out of the door.

After hours spent at the Baylor Plaza Park job site, the day was physically and mentally exhausting for Roderick. He made quick work of six meetings. He still hoped to get home to JaiHonnah and the children before evening. By the time he met with China and Kiran, it was late afternoon.

"Look, Roderick, JR Baylor Holding doesn't want Baylor Industries to go bankrupt, am I right?"

"Yes, that's why I'm going to provide the emergency financial assistance before we default on our interim financing. Kelley has been working very hard to turn around the situation Lionel Porter left the company in. That, coupled with the downturn in the market, and this investment raid, is consuming too much of my time."

"You're facing two immediate deadlines that require assistance from its leading shareholders to avert a disaster. JR Baylor holds twenty-seven percent of Baylor Industries, but the rest is outstanding."

"Yes, and I'm going to leak to the press that the company doesn't believe it can obtain, on commercially reasonable terms, adequate liquidity to support its operations in the near term without substantial credit support from its principal stockholders."

"You're losing your grip, Roderick," China huffed.

"No, he's not," Kiran said slowly, as if something began to occur to her. "You're going to make it appear JR Holding is looking at several options, including equity investments and direct investor loans. If the investors believe that loan guarantees are unlikely, then they'll buy JR Holding because they believe the company is vulnerable to takeover."

"Exactly," said Roderick. "Then I'll issue four or five million shares of common stock when stock prices in Baylor Industries are weak and buy them up under a new corporate structure. With the substantial credit support from all of the principal stockholders, I'll be in the position to obtain adequate bank financing from Nick Collins using all of JR Holding's assets as security."

"Financing will be combined with income from launched insurance claims related to anomalies that forced reconfiguration and then JR Holding will recoup its investment," Kiran said, as she turned to face Roderick. "The old shell game. That's brilliant!"

"Only if it works," Roderick said. "My concern is whether the major stockholders will keep their eyes on the rock and be forced to show their hands."

"They couldn't help it. They'd have to show up," China said.

"Oh, yes they can. Whoever is behind this could send in a proxy, especially if they are offshore, but it's a risk I'm going to take." He glanced at his watch. "Look, I have another appointment.

I believe we know where we stand. Legally, Kiran, am I on solid ground?"

"I thought I had seen it all, but this is a brilliant new approach to the old shell game. I'll have to do some legal research, but I'll get back to you in a couple of days."

"Fine, the sooner the better. I'm out of here."

His pal, Ice, followed Roderick to the car.

"Man, I'm not going to try and pretend I understood anything about what went on in there," he admitted, "but, whatever it was, you look like you were in the zone."

A grin crossed Roderick's lips and curled his mustache. "I am, but I learned from a master of the game," he said, as he eased into his Benz and lowered the convertible top.

"Basketball?" Ice asked in confusion, as he climbed into the car.

"No, business," Roderick answered confidently.

After Roderick and Ice left the hospital from checking on Mallory, Roderick dropped Ice off at the office. Roderick wheeled through traffic and made it home in less than one hour. He was looking forward to a long, leisurely and relaxing evening with

JaiHonnah. Whistling a tune as he entered the house, he pulled off his jacket and loosened his tie.

Suddenly he was struck by the silence. Betterman wasn't in his usual place. The children weren't scampering to meet him at the door and JaiHonnah's smile didn't light up the empty house. He wandered through the huge mansion, but only his movements broke the silence. Roderick noticed the message light blinking on the library telephone. He stared at it for a moment not wanting to hear the inevitable. The front doorbell rang and Roderick answered it.

"Flowers for Mrs. Baylor," the deliveryman said cheerfully. "Sorry, we're a little late delivering these. This place isn't easy to find."

Roderick looked at the box of flowers, reached into his pocket, and tipped the driver. "You married?" he asked.

"Yes," the deliveryman answered with a broad smile. "Seven years."

"Count your blessings. I hope your wife enjoys the flowers."

"Thanks, Mister," the man said with confusion written on his face.

Roderick closed the door and returned to the library. The light was still flashing. He dug his hands deep into his pockets and stood staring at it. The feeling of helplessness was never a part of his demeanor, but his shoulders slumped forward and his head bowed.

Without JaiHonnah, what did it all matter? Without JaiHonnah, why bother to be the best at the game? Had his ego gotten so enormous it blocked out everything else? Everyone else including his wife and family? At that moment, he would have given up the game and all of its excitement just to hold JaiHonnah in his arms. Slowly he turned and walked out of the library.

Chapter Nine

KELLEY HUNG UP THE TELEPHONE AND sat back in her seat, contemplating what Roderick just told her. Most of their conversation centered around the investigations they had conducted on Monique Baylor and Lionel Porter. Other than being at the Cannes Film Festival at the same time, nothing else about Monique's and Lionel's activities was discovered. They had stayed in the same hotel also, but so did hundreds of others. It was all circumstantial, but something still didn't sit well with Kelley. The fact Lionel had his wife, children, and his lover, Monique, with him was less troublesome than Lionel being at the festival at all. *Since when did Lionel develop a taste for the arts?* The telephone buzzer distracted her.

"Yes, Bessie," she answered.

"State Senator Milton Bradshaw is here, Ms. Baylor."

Kelley took a quick look at her watch and grimaced. She had forgotten they planned to go out that night for dinner and dancing. She was supposed to meet him at the restaurant at seven o'clock and it was already eight fifteen.

"I'm on my way out the door now," she said hurriedly.

She opened the door and Milton's stoic expression grew into a devilish smile. "I should be furious with you, lady," he said eying her, "but you're well worth the wait."

Kelley managed a slight smile. Milton Bradshaw, a state senator and successful Georgia businessman, was very handsome and debonair indeed. He was a divorcée, with two grown children, who looked like he should still be on the cover of *Gentleman's Quarterly.* They met when she moved to Georgia and dated frequently until Jake started monopolizing her time. Now, with Jake out of the picture, Milton was pressing hard for a relationship. Milton was patient with her, and she appreciated that, but he wasn't Jake Hawkins.

"Senator," she said, smiling, "public servants are accustomed to waiting for their constituents, are they not?"

"This one is." He smiled, giving her a quick kiss on the lips.

The gesture surprised her. They had not been intimate, but Kelley knew the signals. If the senator had his way, this was going to be an ambiance night. She had not slept with anyone since she walked out on Jake. After the first week of near hourly calls and daily flowers and gifts from Jake, all had ceased. To the best of her knowledge, he had not returned to Atlanta. His townhouse next door to hers remained empty except for a cleaning crew. Though she ached to see him and be with him, she was determined to move on with her life. Milton Bradshaw seemed like a good place to start.

The evening went as she predicted. Milton took her to a very exclusive restaurant for a romantic, candlelit dinner and an evening of dancing. He was very attentive and they were having an enchanting and fun-filled evening. Still, as he held her in his arms on the dance floor and whispered his pleasure in her ear, she wished with all of her heart he was Jake Hawkins. She closed her eyes and swayed to the music. Nothing about Milton's body pressing against hers felt like Jake. Milton's cologne, although expensive, didn't arouse her senses the way Jake's did. The way Milton held her didn't contain the possessive embrace Jake's did. Under ordinary circumstances, Milton would have been her kind of man though, but these weren't ordinary circumstances.

When Milton stopped dancing, Kelley didn't immediately notice the music was still playing. She opened her eyes and looked up at him. His fixed gaze over her shoulder startled her and she turned her head to see the mountain looming behind her.

"That's my woman you're holding, Senator," Jake growled lowly with a decidedly sinister grin.

Kelley stopped breathing, although her heart was slamming against her chest. She turned around slowly in Milton's arms to face Jake.

When Jake walked into the restaurant, he stood in silhouette, watching Kelley on the dance floor with Milton Bradshaw. He resented the way Bradshaw held her in his arms, but her statuesque shape, the sway of her hips, and the fullness of her breasts welded his phallus into a steel-like form. He didn't try to deny what he felt for her. It showed fiercely in his eyes and his demeanor. He was in love again. Deeply in love and the object of his desire was in the arms of another man. The sight of that galvanized within him. That sight had to end.

"Jake," Kelley said, standing with her back against Milton's chest, but a breath away from Jake. "I'm not your woman. Now if you'll excuse us…"

Jake leaned into Milton over Kelley's shoulder and whispered something in his ear that caused Milton's body to go stone still. His arms dropped from around Kelley. Jake took Kelley's arm, leading her ahead of him from the dance floor. They entered the vestibule and the maître d' opened a door to an empty, private, dining room. Once inside, Jake spun Kelley around into his arms and captured her mouth. She was stunned, but his hot, wet, probing tongue nearly caused her to lose control of her resolve. She didn't instantly realize the needful groans were coming from her. Her body came alive and finally she could hold out no longer. She wrapped her arms around his neck and opened to him. Jake's broad, strong hand cupped her butt, pressing her against the hard, long, full pulsating ridge of his body and deepening the ecstasy they shared for what seemed like an eternity. Jake held Kelley's head in his free hand, robbing her of her ability to move or think. Finally, he permitted her to breathe. Stunned at her own need for his touch, she pushed off against his chest.

"Hello, dahlin', I see you missed me, too," he said, his deep male tone full of emotion.

Kelley snapped to her senses. "How dare you waltz in here and...and..." she sputtered, backing away from him, "and embarrass me like this! Who the hell do you think you are?"

A confident grin bordering on arrogance crossed Jake's lips. His eyes smoldered and bore into hers. He took off his designer suit jacket and loosened his tie. Kelley saw the determination in his eyes, as he slowly approached her. She put up her hands to slow his progress, but she ran out of real estate and found herself up against the corner of the walls with nowhere to run.

"I know who I am." He advanced on her. "I'm your man. I'm the man you're going to be living with for the rest of our lives. I'm the man who's going to cater to your every whim, wish, and desire. I'm the man who's got you in his blood. I'm the man who knows what you need, what lights your fire, and fuels your desire." He cornered her. "I'm the man you're going to marry, Kelley Baylor. That's who I am."

Jake put his hands on the walls effectively encasing, but not touching her. He captured Kelley's mouth again.

She turned her head away. "Jake, please."

Jake lathed the hollow of her throat, the exposed area of her shoulder and the swell of her breast.

"Please what, dahlin'?" he crooned against her ear.

Kelley's breath abated with the sensuousness of his aggressive seduction. Her breasts heaved on her unsteady breaths and she trembled slightly.

"Please what?" Jake repeated with a deep groan under her chin.

"Please stop what you're doing to me," she said weakly.

"Never," he groaned, as he possessed her again in another searing kiss.

Then he broke it off and backed away from her.

"Wedding's going to be in a week or two at Hawk House, soon as I take care of a little business. I've arranged for a flight to bring your family to Hawkinstown for the ceremony. I also bought one of those bridal shops on my way here. Left the deed at your office with your secretary. Go pick out one of them pretty wedding gowns and trousseau. Pack for warm weather. Sell your townhouse and your car." He slipped back into his jacket. "Clear up any loose ends at your company and appoint someone to take your place." He straightened his tie. "Oh, and make sure your passport is current. You got all of that, dahlin'?" He grinned.

Kelley was stunned. "No! You need medical attention!" she flashed. "I'm not going anywhere with you, Jake Hawkins! I have a business to run and a life to live and it doesn't include you!"

A sly, dangerous grin crossed Jake's face. "You mean you *had* a business to run. After I finish my business, your business is finished. Baylor will belong to BlackHawk and you, dahlin', will belong to me." He winked at her. "Y'all have a nice day, ya hear?" he said, as he slipped out of the door. Then he ducked his head back in. "And about the Senator, send the boy toy home. My chauffeur will be waiting for you."

Jake was gone, but his presence lingered. Kelley sat down heavily in a near stupor. Moments later, when the haze cleared, she leapt to her feet. She had to get to Roderick and fast.

JaiHonnah saw to the loading of the luggage in the rented van and made sure the children were securely fastened in their safety seats before she turned to Jacob.

"Are you sure you don't want to come home to Texas with me, Jai? I mean, it's hot as blazes here in New Mexico this time of the year and you're due to deliver that kid of yours any day now."

"I am home, Jacob. I need to spend some time with *Shimá sâni.*"

"All right, if you insist, but consider carefully what I've told you. I'll send a jet for you when you get enough of this heat."

He kissed her on her forehead and left. JaiHonnah got behind the wheel of the van and drove to Ship Rock. When she arrived, Kiavi, her grandmother, came out of the adobe to greet her and the children.

"*Ya'ha'teeh, Shimá sâni,*" she said, addressing her grandmother, with tears rolling down her face.

"*Bienvenido.* The pain, it is great, no?" Kiavi asked, wiping JaiHonnah's tears with her fingers.

"Very great, *Shimá sâni.* The dreams, they scare me. I need to be with Skai," she said stoically.

"You need to see the Shaman for answers," Kiavi said, completing her thought.

JaiHonnah nodded in agreement. "I'm losing my husband."

"Come, child, we will speak of this thing when you have brought forth this new life."

JaiHonnah and the children entered the adobe.

"Any way you cut it, Roderick, you're screwed," Kiran said, looking over the reports of the takeover. "BlackHawk owns seventy-three percent of JR Baylor voting stock. You and JaiHonnah together hold twenty-seven percent. BlackHawk has the right to call the shots now. They've called for a stockholders meeting on Friday in Hawkinstown."

Roderick paced the room with his head down and hands in his pockets. "Fine. I'll be there."

Kiran looked at him curiously. "Look, Baylor, you're taking this all too calmly for my comfort. You aren't contemplating any criminal action, are you?"

Roderick stopped pacing and looked at Kiran. "Only that which could be considered justifiable homicide. There's a dead man walking around controlling my life, threatening my family. It's going to end on Friday in Hawkinstown. Bone up on your Texas criminal law, counselor, you're going to need it."

"Baylor, that's not justifiable homicide you're contemplating. It's premeditated. I'd strongly suggest you take some time and consider the consequences. You could lose not only your wife and family, but also your life."

"You don't understand, Kiran. My wife and family *are* my life. Without them, nothing else matters. Not the business, not the projects, not even being the best at the game. I've left myself exposed for that very reason. I want to know who is doing this and I want this over with. I want my wife and my family back. I'll be content to live in a one-room shack, if I have them with me."

"Then you haven't heard from them?"

"No. Nothing. Not a word. It's been weeks. I've called, but Jacob tells me she's not available. He doesn't even pretend he's not enjoying this, but even that doesn't matter. I had made up my mind when she left that I would sell the business or let it go bankrupt."

"What changed your mind?"

"Something my father said before he died."

"What was that?"

"He told me to make it better. Now I have a way to do that. I have BlackHawk right where I want them."

"Exactly where is that?" Kiran asked with a puzzled expression.

"An unguarded moment," he said firmly.

The jet touched down on the private runway at BlackHawk ranch, Jake Hawkins' sprawling estate in Hawkinstown. Roderick strode to the waiting limo with confidence and purpose. Kiran and Ice scrambled after him and climbed in. Roderick's stomach churned, belying his outwardly cool exterior. He felt the emptiness, the loss of his center. His gut wrenched with love for JaiHonnah. He craved her more and more every day. She controlled his every waking and sleeping moment. His loins ached for her and her caress. No matter what was before them, if he could win her back, never would he let his need to be the master of the game interfere with his all-consuming love for her.

He sat stoically, not breathing hard, awaiting the sight of her. The monstrously large Hawk House loomed up as they came over the ridge. The long, red brick driveway to the house, under the sheltering arms of large, old-growth trees, permitted only dappled sunlight to filter through. Yet, Roderick could see Jake leaning against one of the tall, round pillars of the wide veranda. His hands were in his pockets, his Stetson pulled low on his head just above his eyes, and a cigarillo clenched in his teeth. His poker face gave no warning of what was to come.

"Where is she?" Roderick asked without preliminaries or pleasantries as soon as he left the limo.

"'Spose you mean my daughter?" Jake asked, rolling the cigarillo around between his teeth.

"I mean my wife!" Roderick said with vehemence.

"Man can't handle his woman, can't be much of a man." Jake glared at him.

"Man enough to take you on and win," Roderick said, climbing the stairs to stand toe-to-toe with Jake, "but this isn't about that."

Jake grinned. "Hold the thought, boy. You're going to need it when I'm finished with you, but, for the moment, I have more pressing business to discuss with you."

"Nothing is more important to me than my wife and family," he growled.

"*My* life is more important to me at the moment, boy!" Jake bellowed.

The statement took Roderick by surprise and Jake noticed him blink.

"No such luck, Baylor. I'm not dying and I'm in the prime of my life."

Jake walked toward Kiran and Ice. "Go on in the house and make yourselves at home. I want to talk to the boy privately."

Ice and Kiran looked toward Roderick, who nodded in agreement. They entered the house while Jake walked down the steps. Roderick followed. They walked the ranch together silently both with heads up, shoulders back, and hands dug deep into their pockets.

When they reached the corral, Jake turned and faced Roderick. "Son, I built this place from the ground up with my bare hands. I fought off the Klan, the carpetbaggers, the glory seekers, the pious and the positioned. Against all odds, I built me an empire. I'm not a greedy man. I took my share of what this country promised I could have if I obeyed the rules and worked hard—freedom and liberty. Had to fight for that, too—just like you. I gave back what I could, but it was never enough. Money and power are never enough for men like us, like you and me. That's not what makes us the best that we can be. The love of a good woman takes us that extra mile. Propels us into that zone you basketball players are always talking about. That's what makes us get up every morning with a smile on our faces and sends us to bed each night with one purpose in mind—pleasing our women.

"I've known the love of a good woman before and I lost her. I fathered four children with Skai. One daughter was stolen away from the clinic the day she was born, but I haven't given up looking for her. I made mistakes with my other three children. At least with JaiHonnah, things are turning out good for her. God knows why, but she's in love with you and I believe you love her, too.

"With Adam, well, I stopped him from pursuing a career he wanted on the race car circuit. It was pure selfishness on my part. I didn't want him hurt or killed in some auto accident. I also stopped him from pursuing a relationship with your friend, Vivian Alexander Jackson. I loved that girl like a daughter and would have welcomed her into this family. Yet, because I believed she was in love with Chuck Montgomery, I got into it to stop it and I was right. That doesn't make me feel vindicated because Adam is still heartsick. One day I hope he will heal and find a woman who can return his love. I know my son loves me. That's the only reason he stuck out working in the family business all these years, but this isn't a challenge for him. Eventually he'll want to go his own way and I'll let him because I love him more than I can say.

"Jacob, well, he is a completely different story. Unlike JaiHonnah and Adam, Jacob won't let himself be loved or love any woman. He's still angry because his mother died and he blames me for that. While I was building an empire, I let my family fare for themselves. My wife, Skai, took care of all of us, but not herself. I didn't realize what was going on with her until it was too late. Jacob may never be able to forgive me for that, but I've made peace with it.

"I love my family," he continued, "but they're grown now. I need someone I can love and who can love me in return. I've found that kind of love again and I don't intend to lose it. I want to marry your sister, but that's not going to happen unless you tell her that it's all right. You, boy, hold the key to my happiness, my life is in your hands, and before we go into that house to do battle, as you and I know we must do, I want your answer."

Roderick was floored. Jake had spoken with such honesty, integrity, and sincerity it reached into his soul. He knew what Jake felt. He knew what he had to know about the man. Only one question remained and he asked it.

"Do you love her?"

"More than my next breath."

"Then we understand each other. No matter what goes on between us today, JaiHonnah and Kelley are not in the middle of our war."

"Done." Jake extended his hand.

Roderick firmly shook it and they silently returned to the house.

All conversation ceased in the large, spacious library when Jake and Roderick walked in. Everyone stared at their stoic expressions. Kelley rose from her seat and went immediately to Roderick.

"Little brother," she said, searching his face for a slight smile. "We'll go through this together just like we always have. After today, we can start over, maybe in a different business."

"Do you love him, Kelley?" Roderick asked, searching her eyes.

Kelley looked away and Roderick had his answer.

"I love you, Kelley, but you're fired. You're no longer a part of any Baylor enterprise."

Kelley's eyes widened in shock and disbelief. Roderick put one hand to her troubled face and caressed her. "Marry the old buzzard and be happy. You deserve better, but what do I know, I'm only your little brother."

Tears streamed down Kelley's face. "He's a hawk, not a buzzard," she said, smiling slightly through her pained expression.

"Same difference." He smiled. "He's still trying to pick my bones clean."

Kelley buried her face in Roderick's chest.

"Let's get this over with," Jake bellowed. "I've got some more living to do."

Everyone moved to seats around a conference table. Jake sat at the head of the table with Jacob on his left and Roderick on his right. Adam sat next to Jacob and Kelley sat next to Roderick. Kirin and Ice sat in chairs arranged behind Roderick. Other major stockholders filled the remaining seats at the table, except three empty seats at the opposite end.

"The meeting of BlackHawk Holding will now come to order. A quorum is present and we will proceed to the first order of business, which is the acquisition of JR Baylor Holding and its subsidiaries."

"Mr. President, may I suggest we postpone the discussion on the Baylor acquisition until after we have completed discussions regarding the sale of BlackHawk stock to JR Baylor Limited?" Roderick asked.

Those gathered sat in stunned silence.

Jacob Junior's voice sliced the tense air. "What makes you think that you can waltz in here and take over BlackHawk?" Jacob thundered. "This is a family matter that doesn't include you, Baylor!"

"Family?" Roderick questioned derisively. "You think being a part of *this* family is some type of license to steal my company?"

"The stock was for sale on the open market and I bought it!" Jacob railed.

"What did you pay for it?" Roderick asked. "What did it cost me?"

"A few sleepless nights without me, I hope," JaiHonnah said, entering the room with Kiavi and Ezra.

Everyone's head turned toward her and Kiavi holding a small baby in her arms. Roderick quickly rose from the table and rounded it to reach JaiHonnah. She held him off with one hand.

"Not so fast, Mr. Baylor," she said with strength of purpose.

Roderick stopped in his tracks. He wanted to hold her too slender body in his arms, but something in her demeanor stopped him cold. His eyes went from her to his baby. He gently lifted the small bundle from Kiavi's arms.

"It is a girl child," Kiavi said, as she handed the baby to Roderick. "Nine pounds."

Roderick's eyes smiled, as he viewed the beautiful details of his daughter's face. He was so engrossed he didn't notice JaiHonnah had walked away from him. When he looked up again to see her, he caught the powerful slap she laid across Jacob Junior's face.

"You are my brother, Jacob, and I do love you. God forgive me, but I could learn to hate you for what you tried to do to me, my husband, and my family!" she spat with venom. "First, you force down the market and then you buy up the stock below value using my RAMOS trust account, without my knowledge or authorization, as an offshore holding company. Using my account, you were trying to make it appear I was in on this scheme of yours.

"You didn't care how bad you made me or my company look while you're doing it," she continued. "Or, how you made it appear that it was me who was attempting a hostile takeover of my husband's company.

"Then you come to me and tell me that my husband is having an illicit affair with my doctor and expect me to give you my stock in BlackHawk and JR Baylor Industries so that you can wage a war against him. *'To teach him a lesson,'* you told me.

"Well, understand this, my brother, my faith in my husband and in the future of his company remains strong. I've turned over my proxy in BlackHawk Holding to him, without his knowledge or consent, and you can't do a thing to stop me. I'll fight you and anyone else by my husband's side!"

She glared at Jacob and then her father. "It's too bad this family has not known joy since the death of my mother instead of the insidious and relentless drive for wealth and power!" She took her directed stare from Jake back to Jacob. "My only question of you, brother, is why? What have I done to you that you should treat me as your enemy?"

Jacob Junior's black eyes blazed with sudden anger. "Because you, little sister, were the chosen one! The one mother and father prized the most and then you married him!" He pointed an arrow-straight finger at Roderick. "A common person! You are a Hawkins! A daughter of Navajo!" His chest rose and fell in rage. "He is undeserving! He is not Navajo—not a son of Hawk!"

"But you are!" Jake's voice boomed. "Yet, you sought to overthrow me! You sought to ascend to the top because you are a Hawkins! Because I love you and you are of your mother's womb and my body! Not because you worked to earn that status, but because you thought it was yours for the taking."

"I have worked, father! I have labored day and night for BlackHawk! I deserve to lead it! It is time you step down! You have let your liaison with *that* woman," he pointed at Kelley, "control you!"

The air was charged with static, but everyone sat perfectly still in wonder and disbelief.

"Is that why you tried to destroy her? Or was it more?" Jake bellowed. "You used everyone at your disposal to get to Kelley Baylor through her brother! You knew she would rise to her brother's defense and go down with him if it had to be so because the Baylors are dedicated to their family unit! You wanted to drive a wedge between her and me, but you forgot...I invented the game you tried to play.

"I gave you specific instructions that Baylor was off limits to any aggression on the part of BlackHawk, but you went behind my back!" he continued. "You started this insidious backdoor hostile takeover attempt using your sister's company to do it behind her back. Something I would never do. If I'm going to fight for something, I look a man in the eye and tell him what I'm going to do. I don't try to stab him in the back the way you have tried to do. You dishonored me!

"You tried to drive your brother out of the company because you knew he would not go along with you and your plan. He had the family's and the company's best interest at heart! You tried to drive a wedge between your sister and her husband!"

He snapped his finger and Ezra ushered Lionel Porter, Monique Baylor, Calvin Chapman, Rothman Childs, and Levi Hall, aka, Killer—all of the co-conspirators—into the room. Then he continued.

"You brought these people together secretly in Europe and plotted the destruction of Roderick Baylor. You bankrolled Lionel Porter and then knocked him from power to lure Baylor into overextending himself to buy Porter's company. You and Calvin encouraged Monique to threaten Baylor with the loss of his daughters to keep his mind off his work. You used Childs to cut off

Baylor's primary source of financial support. Finally, you used this overgrown adolescent, Killer, aka Levi Hall, to sabotage Baylor's work sites. You sought to destroy him in my eyes because you knew I respected him! I respected another man's business acumen, but I loved you! And still he beat you again at your own game!

"You paid for a worthless company! A shell! The oldest game in the business. Baylor traded everything he owned in exchange for BlackHawk stock. Only a street kid would know how to do that! Someone who's had to live by his wits in the real world! While you were jet-setting all over the world, whoring in my footsteps to gain information from the women I bedded, he was in the streets learning how to be the master of the game! He worked side by side with his workers. He didn't ask anyone to give him a damn thing. He's kept his eyes on the prize while you kept your eyes on my wallet!"

Jacob puffed and exploded. "All my life it has been *your* company! Go here, Jacob! Go there, Jacob! Take this company and run it! Acquire that one! Still it is *your* company! Not *our* company! I've lived in your shadow! Picked up your crumbs! In all of those years, you never came to me and said, here, this will all be yours some day!" His black eyes narrowed like a cat ready to pounce. "I hated you for that! Now that you want to leave the company, it's not me—your son, your own flesh and blood, your flunky, your lap dog—you want to install as the head of BlackHawk, is it, father?"

"No, it isn't. You had a better chance than any man to head BlackHawk, but whoever heads it must put family first! That person must have integrity, not just business savvy! The name BlackHawk means something in this country. It means a man from the swamps of Nowhere, Louisiana, can rise to control his own destiny. Something I failed to teach you, or you failed to learn. Well, you'll have plenty of time to ponder that lesson!"

He turned to the astonished faces around the table and looked each one squarely in the eyes. "I have called to order this meeting and a quorum is present. The first order of business will be the selection of a new chairman and chief executive officer for BlackHawk Holding. Do I hear a nomination?"

"Mr. Chairman," Adam began, "I nominate J. Roderick Baylor for the chairmanship," he said, as he also whispered across the table to Roderick, "I'm not such a fool as you might think."

"Do I hear a second?" Jake bellowed.

"I second that nomination," JaiHonnah spoke up.

"It has been moved and seconded. Call the question. All opposed signify by raising your hand. Seeing no hands raised, the motion is carried. J. Roderick Baylor, you are now Chairman and Chief Executive Officer of BlackHawk. Wear that title well," Jake said, extending his hand, "or this old hawk will rise like a Phoenix from the ashes to take it away from you."

Everything had proceeded so quickly Roderick barely had time to react. He stood holding his daughter in his arms and shook Jake's hand. Then he turned to Jacob Junior and extended his hand to him.

"Good game," Roderick said. "Welcome to the new team. You will run BlackHawk as President, Jacob. There are no more mountains left for me to climb. With you on my right, Adam on my left, Ice at my back and JaiHonnah as my center, we have an unbeatable team. Let's make it the dream team together."

Jacob Junior rose from his seat and slowly extended his hand. "There's always next year," he said stoically.

Roderick's grin curled his lips. "Call me, JRock. All of my competitors do. Get a ball and meet me on the court. I'll show you a little something about how to play the game. It will keep me sharp." Jacob Junior nodded and Roderick turned to Jake. "What are you going to do now?"

Jake gathered Kelley to his chest and gently kissed her lips.

"Well, boy, if the rest of your family has arrived, in a few minutes I'm going to marry your sister. Then we're going to Africa. President of these United States thinks I'd make a pretty decent Ambassador. Apparently, Vivian spoke to the President and to the powers that be on the African continent while she was there on her honeymoon. When she met with the President, she made a strong suggestion that he and I, together—my resources and his—could make things better. Tarnation, I might have to end up adopting that judge! She's got more hawk in her than I do, but boy, it's about those secret negotiations you sent her to Africa to handle. Now just how does this Adopt-a-City exchange program work?"

"How did you find out about that?" Roderick asked, surprised. "I know Vivian would not have told you."

"The eyes of Texas have been upon you for a very long time, boy. I watched you dribble your first ball in college and then professionally. Even bought a piece of the team because of you. Now, explain this new program."

"Baylor Plaza Park will become a trade enterprise zone and will adopt an African village to begin direct trade and commerce with them exclusively. We teach them our skills and they teach us theirs. Exchange cultures and handcrafted cultural artifacts and other precious resources. This program grew out of Vivian's and my desire to fund a new type of education system for the children in Baylor Park Academy. It's based on the system created by Vivian's father in the Village of Goodwill, Summer County, South Carolina. Dr. Roselyn Hunter Greenfield will head the school and work closely with Vivian's father. If the program works, other segments of the city will join. I hope to interest other cities in the program. Now that you're going to be the ambassador, this is what you can do to facilitate this process—"

"Oh, no you don't," JaiHonnah interrupted. "If you two start getting your heads together over business, Kelley's wedding dress won't get worn today and I won't get to sleep with my husband tonight. It's been six weeks since I slept with him. Tonight he's mine."

Jake and Roderick eyed each other. "The hell you say!" They laughed in unison.

Later that night after the wedding, Roderick and JaiHonnah put little Skai Littlefeather Baylor to bed in her bassinet in their bedroom suite. Roderick draped his arms around JaiHonnah and pulled her back to his chest. Then he extended her away from him, spun her around to face him, and asked the question that had plagued him for hours. "Jai, how did you know? About the plan to ruin me, I mean."

She shrugged listlessly. "You wouldn't believe me if I told you."

"Try me."

A few moments passed while she gathered her thoughts. Touching her head briefly, she struggled with rational contemplation. "It came to me in a dream. On my flight to Washington from Italy. A vision I had even before I met you."

Roderick looked at her incredulously. "A dream?"

"Yes. You see, my mother used to have visions or visitations. See things before they happened. It was a gift from the Old Ones, the Ancestors. My *Shimá sâni* told me, as a child, I used to have visions, too, just like my mother. This time I was on the night flight coming to America to meet with you for the first time. In the dream we were standing on the barren ground, facing each other, but the earth between me and a man was separating us. There was a hawk on the man's shoulder digging its talons into his flesh. I was screaming, but the land kept shifting me further apart from the man. I didn't know who the man was. All I knew was I loved him and something terrible was happening to us. Then, suddenly,

I heard him whisper, *'Let yourself go, baby. Relax. I'm here with you. No one but us, Jai. No one in the universe, but you and me.'* That voice. Now I know it was your soul somehow reaching out to me, comforting me and I knew we would be all right. The Ancestors had heard my pleas and would protect us from harm."

"Do you always have these visions, these dreams?"

Slowly she shook her head. "No, not often. Sometimes years will pass between the visions, but when they come, they seem like an omen, a warning. I had those visions when I thought I was losing you. The visions were strong and frightening. That's why I had to leave you. I had to go to see the Shaman to help me interpret the dreams." She looked up into his eyes. "I would do anything to keep from losing you. I love you."

Roderick kissed her gently. "You could never lose me, Jai. I'm in love with you. I belong to you completely." He kissed her neck and her shoulder and ran his hands lovingly over her milk-swollen breasts and her flat abdomen. "Nine pounds?" he whispered against her ear. "How sore are you now?" he groaned, his voice thick with passion.

"I think I can handle the rock, but I haven't found a condom I think will fit you yet." She took several sizes and types out of the pocket of her scant robe and held them up.

Roderick released her and looked into her eyes. "Uh, Jai, you're joking right?" Confusion clouded his face. "I swear to you, I haven't been with another woman. I didn't sleep with Savannah. You want me to wear a condom?"

A wry grin curled her lips. "I know you haven't slept with another woman, but either you start wearing condoms, you fine, sexy, tall sip of hot chocolate or you'd better get some rhythm in your stroke. I'm not carrying around a basketball in my stomach every year just because I can't stay off the rock."

She pushed him backward onto the bed and mounted him. Then she began measuring the condoms against his phallus. Roderick confidently laced his fingers behind his head and waited, enjoying the sight and the sensations of his wife trying to fit a condom on him. When JaiHonnah had opened the last packet and discarded it in frustration, she looked up at the smug expression on Roderick's face.

"None of them fit," she fussed.

"I could have told you that. Only one glove fits me," he said, lifting her onto his engorged shaft. "And you have it, you sexy little mother."

JaiHonnah trembled with ecstasy, as she enveloped him. There was no need for preliminaries, as Roderick reversed their positions. Prepared for him, JaiHonnah rotated her hips and thrust upward against him. Roderick moved his hips against her like a jackhammer in slowed motion, deeper and deeper. Every muscle and fiber of their bodies went into the joining. Fire met fire and blazed between them for what seemed like an eternity. Something beyond them took control and the sweet ecstasy took them to rapture.

"Roderick!" JaiHonnah gasped repeatedly.

"I know, baby. It'll be all right. Nine months will pass quickly." Roderick trembled and strained against the release, but he exploded deep inside her. "I'm moving our office to Deer Haven. This time we'll do this together. I don't want you out of my reach for one moment. This baby will see my face first when he's born."

They were swept to the place where babies were made and another unguarded moment passed.

Chapter Ten

"JAKE?" KELLEY SNUGGLED UP TO HER brand new husband, in his gigantic bed, at his BlackHawk ranch in Hawkinstown.

"Yes, dahlin'?" He hugged her closer and kissed her temple.

"When did you know you wanted to marry me?"

"Don't rightly know the answer to that. When I first saw you at your brother's office, I knew I wanted you. You were so beautiful that something tripped on a need I hadn't felt since I lost Skai. All during the time I met with your brother and met his daughters, your nieces, I couldn't get you out of my head.

"I've had women, more than my share," he continued, "but I couldn't look at another one after I met you. Then when I got a taste of you, nothing was the same for me. So I have to say the first time I laid eyes on you, I wanted you something fierce."

Kelley looked up into Jake's eyes. "It was pretty much the same for me that first time, too. I saw a real man and I was so infatuated with you. I couldn't allow myself to fall for you though. I tried to fight my feelings for you, but it didn't work. I fell in love with you, Jake Hawkins."

"That's okay, dahlin'. I'm in love with you, too."

"You'll have to be patient with me. I've never been a wife before, but you've been a husband."

"I wasn't the best husband and Skai and our children suffered for it. Someone took our daughter out of that clinic days after she was born. Then I lost Skai to breast cancer because I was so busy building my business. I left Skai alone too often to tend to our family by herself. I don't intend to make the same mistake twice. I turned the company over to your brother because he is truly the best person to head it. With JaiHawk at his side, they'll do extremely well as a team.

"Now I only have being an ambassador and loving my wife to contend with."

"What about Jacob, Junior, and what he tried to do to you?"

"He's still my son and I love him, just as I love all of my children, but he's never met a challenge like your brother before.

When Roderick made him president of the company, I could see something turn on in his eyes. He's still competitive, but Roderick has given him the respect he failed to feel when he worked for me. I'm not saying he won't try to manipulate the situation again. After all, he is my son and I trained him, but I haven't cut the ties that bind completely. I will continue to keep a watchful eye on the situation, but no one or nothing is going to stop me from enjoying being your husband, Kelley Hawkins."

"I love the sound of that, Jake. I plan to enjoy being your wife and learning my role as the wife of an ambassador. I want you to be proud of me."

"As long as you love me, dahlin', nothing else could make me happier, except maybe one thing."

"Finding your daughter."

"Yes."

"I'll include her in my prayers."

"Thank you, dahlin'," he said and kissed her. His prayers were also full of the need to find LaiLoni Skai, but if the dream or vision he experienced on JaiHonnah's wedding day was any indication, he would see his daughter again.

Epilogue

A LONE FIGURE, FLEET OF foot, swiftly ran a deserted, mountainous roadway toward the rising sun. Time was running out.

ABOUT THE AUTHOR

Ann Jeffries, the critically acclaimed author of the Family Reunion—Wisdom of the Ancestors Series, is a native of Washington, DC. As an only child, she enjoyed the benefits of a private school education at Allen in Asheville, North Carolina and a public education at the University of Maryland. Ann began writing fiction for her own amusement.

Ms. Jeffries is the recipient of many awards for leadership and public service. A keynote speaker at colleges, universities, conference, and conventions, she has extensively traveled the North American continent, Asia and Europe. Among other endeavors, she is an entrepreneur, an avid supporter of public television and live theatre, a genealogist, and a voracious reader.

Her pride and joy are her family, particularly her Fabulous Four grands. She lives in Maryland and South Carolina.

Follow Ann on her website: www.annjeffries.net, Facebook @Ann Jeffries, on Twitter @ Ann Jeffries, and her publishing house site: www.newviewliterature.com. Her novels are available in both e-book and paperback formats and will soon be available in audio on Audible, iTunes, and Amazon. Autographed copies can be found through annjeffries.net and also un autographed on Amazon.com and barnesandnoble.com.